THE BLOODSTONE LEGACY

HERE THEY LIE

D.K. BURROW

www.dkburrow.com

Cover Design by: Regina Wamba of MaeIDesign.com

For Madeline, Nicholas, and Steve

Chapter One
༄༅

Reese

Aunt Kate had picked a bad time to die.

My healthier-than-most-Olympians great-aunt just had to pass away on her front porch three weeks shy of her hundredth birthday. One minute my mother was fretting from her hospital bed—trying to decide how to explain to my aunt that thanks to the hit-and-run, we'd have to postpone our planned trip to Georgia—and the next the phone rang and we didn't need to make the trip anymore. I wasn't going to be heading back to my hometown with a truck full of streamers and supplies for the party. I was still on my way to Georgia, but now I was heading there with bins, crates, and boxes. The kind of supplies needed to help settle her estate.

Funny how a single phone call could change absolutely everything.

So now I was on my way out of New Orleans to the city I'd last visited when I was in grade school. Dad couldn't make the trip. With Mom out of commission, someone had to keep the family businesses running. At least the businesses we admitted to.

Estate sales by day, ghost tours by night. No one in New Orleans batted an eye at the combination. Mom couldn't help with either until the cast came off. Something about a barely mobile guide made a ghost tour less than foreboding.

1

We couldn't have that.

The Everett family was all about making sure our customers didn't leave without goosebumps on their arms, combined with enough creepy memories to keep them up for the next few nights. From the first *good evening* of the night to a black dress and a little white pancake makeup, we set the tone right from the start.

The lawyer's secretary had assured us that I wouldn't be working alone. Kate had anticipated her time was drawing short, and she'd arranged for someone to assist me—a local guy.

Just what I needed.

I'd already tried to explain that I preferred to work alone, but Mrs. Smith had insisted. Kate had made her instructions to Mr. Rose crystal clear. As soon as I arrived in town, I could expect a visit from my new assistant.

So it seemed my first task would involve firing the paid help. Definitely the perfect way to endear myself to the locals. I thudded my head against the seatback. I wasn't heading to Devil's Vale to make friends anyway.

The truck jerked to the right. These roads really sucked. I tugged the wheel back to pull back onto the road I wasn't even sure counted as a road anymore. If I managed to drive off the pavement, I was going to be toast. My GPS had gotten lost an hour ago.

I'd remembered the roads twisted and turned around here, but this was ridiculous. Somewhere a surveyor made a fortune customizing the roads to circumvent property lines. I hope he had to drive these roads in the dark.

It was a nightmare.

"Just go through Millen and hop off 25 onto 21." Mom had spoken with such confidence when she was discussing my route. Easy as pie. So far, the only simple part of the drive was missing the exit onto 21. At some point, the sign had decided it was much better suited to playing hide-and-seek than marking the actual exit to the highway. The only way I found the right road was after I turned around when I was just twenty miles outside of Waynesboro.

I hadn't passed another car for at least a half hour. I drove. And drove. And kept driving. Through the day and into the afternoon. Now edging toward the time of night when the shopkeepers flicked their open signs to closed and locked up. I'd been to towns like Devil's Vale. At night, they turned into ghost towns. No one would be around to welcome me home by the time I pulled into Kate's driveway.

I'd hoped to hit this part of the drive before it even thought about getting dark. If I hadn't missed the turn, I would have made it. Dr. Savage was all about his future anthropologists keeping to schedules. In a random village in the shadow of Mayan ruins, making sure we were aware of the time could save our lives. I didn't know driving to Georgia could be just as harrowing.

Just when I'd finally gotten used to driving through the encroaching darkness, while the woods seemed to be trying to come out and grab my truck, a faint hint of mist appeared in front of me, silvery in the headlights.

The temperature in the cab felt like it dropped ten degrees. From the depths of his crate, Franklin hissed in annoyance. Toss in some creepy organ music, and I was in the opening scene of a horror movie.

The fog seemed to be playing with me, hanging just ahead of my truck until it suddenly wasn't. The silvery whiteness enveloped me. I'd crossed into a weird weather no man's land. The trees were gone. The ditch was gone. The road had disappeared.

As if on cue, the engine sputtered three times before a loud bang preceded total silence—no engine noise, no lingering hum from the radio, not even a sound from anything wild in the trees. Absolute silence.

The fog crept along the ground, suffocating all the noise that should have been around the truck. Or that's how it seemed.

But that was ridiculous. Fog couldn't have made everything disappear.

When I opened the door, I got no help from the overhead dome light. So much for the four hundred dollars I spent on a complete tune up yesterday. If I had to get this piece of junk towed, I was going to send Red-E-Lube my bill.

And I knew just enough about car maintenance to be dangerous.

My cell phone was in the cup holder, and I woke it with a swipe of my thumb. No bars. Figured. Why would I need something like cell phone reception?

I readily admitted to scaring easily, but only if something was breathing.

If the thing going bump in the night was dead, that was another story entirely. Give me a full-bodied apparition anytime. Just hold the snakes.

Maybe I'd just overworked the engine. Just five minutes ago, I'd pleaded with the air conditioner in the truck to find a setting lower than low. That could have made the truck overheat. And Dad always got onto me about not paying attention to all the little details of driving—like how much gas was left in the tank.

I hopped down from the driver's seat and circled to the front of the car before hesitantly reaching for the hood. I'd never hoped for something to burn my hand before. But no, it was ice cold.

With no sign of a knight in a rusty tow truck on the way, I would to have to take matters into my own hands. If I waited for someone to drive by, I'd probably be waiting here tomorrow.

I switched my phone to flashlight mode since that was all it seemed good for at the moment and shone the beam of light into the cavern of mechanicalness, not overly surprised that nothing really stuck out and yelled *I'm broken* to me. Still, my choices were sitting in the driver's seat—trying not to think about needing a bathroom—or pretending to fix my engine. I twisted, wiggled, and checked to make sure the battery cables were still connected.

Nothing seemed wrong.

My cat's deep snore came from inside the cab. I hoped it was a snore. Because if Franklin wasn't asleep, he was laughing at me.

A finger of fog snaked along the ground and gripped my ankle, sending a metallic chill rushing up my leg. I beat a hasty retreat back to the driver's seat.

That's when I first heard it—an engine, out there somewhere. Not close, but not echo-y enough to be on another road.

Even if it stayed hidden, I could tell a car was out there, rumbling in this direction. The fog choked out even the slightest hint of light from headlamps. I stayed in the truck waiting.

One second, I was listening to the hum of an engine somewhere far away, and the next, the headlights were almost married to my bumper. Brakes squealed, and a black sports car came to a stop about a whisker's width from my truck.

"Are you trying to get hit?" A male voice yelled as a car door slammed. The owner of the voice was almost right on top of me before I saw him.

I wished I hadn't.

Tall. Dark. More than a hint muscular.

The kind of guy who looked like he spent hours in the garage bonding with his car. Between the glare on his face and the sleeveless, stained hoodie, he was also the kind of guy who reminded me to lock my doors in downtown New Orleans. He was the definition of what my father would call a very bad idea.

Unfortunately, he was also the closest thing I had to any salvation.

"Why the hell didn't you pull off the road?" He paused, his face hovering just inches from my own.

"My truck kind of decided for me. One minute I'm driving, and the next it's doing an impression of a really large rock."

"What's wrong with it?"

"If I knew that, I wouldn't be sitting here."

That should have been his cue to take a peek under the hood. Instead, his eyes simply swept the ground, and he stomped his feet like a nervous horse.

"You can't stay out here." More stomping. His jerky movements made it look like he was attempting to kick the fog away. "You'll have to get someone to look at it in the morning. It's too dark right now."

"I have a flashlight."

"Like that's going to help. And it's a phone." He spoke with a knife-sharp edge. "We'd better just go."

6

Devil's Vale was a nice, safe, sleepy Georgia town. Small southern towns were supposed to be filled with helpful, neighborly people, weren't they? But I managed to get the one dude who had an attitude like a guy who got kicked out a fraternity for bad behavior. I'd known a fair number of frat boys. That took talent. "But you didn't even look. Can you try jumping it?"

"I'm not going to be able to do anything." He was already backing toward his a-little-too-well-restored sports car. The hairs on the back of my neck stood up. He was from around here. He looked like he probably played football, boxed, or lifted weights for fun.

This guy was scared of the dark?

"I can give you a ride into town."

Please don't let him be a serial killer. He didn't look nice enough to be a serial killer. They always looked like the guys who went door-to-door hoping to give you a Bible. This guy didn't have the nice-guy vibe written on any part of him.

I paused, just as my feet touched the ground. "Can I bring my cat?"

"You have a cat?"

"Well, yeah." I couldn't leave Franklin. "He's in a carrier."

"Okay." Dude didn't look convinced. "I guess you can't just leave him here."

I reached into floorboard to grab Franklin's crate while my rescuer made sounds like I was stalling while the Titanic sank beneath our feet.

"Can you hurry up?"

"Just a second." I'd wedged the carrier in the open space in the passenger's seat floorboard after I fed Franklin

7

dinner. I hadn't been trying for a new permanent home, but it seemed like I might have done it. "It's just stuck or something."

I tugged. I jumped and hit my head on the steering wheel when the guy put his hand in the small of my back.

"Move." He gave the command like he expected me to comply. A not-too-gentle shove further established the idea I needed to move. Once I was out of the way, he reached into the truck. Plastic clicked, and Franklin's crate dangled from his hand. "Here."

"Oh, wait." I stopped mid-step. He didn't try to muffle the stream of curse words leaking through his gritted teeth, but he also didn't hurl me into his car. "One more thing." I scurried back to the truck and grabbed my bag from the passenger seat. I might currently be a damsel in distress, but tomorrow morning I'd be a damsel in distress with a toothbrush. "Thanks."

"Thank me after we get out of here." Without doing the gentlemanly-holding-a-car-door-open-for-a-girl thing, he practically jumped back behind the driver's seat of his car.

I followed.

"Might want to hold on." He pressed the accelerator, and my stomach churned with the question of whether or not I should have just stayed back with my truck. I had a pillow. I could have slept there.

He revved the engine, and we sped off faster than I'd ever dream of attempting in my truck. Of course, he was used to the woods, the twisting roads, and the way the trees seemed to close in.

The car began to bounce, and for a minute I was caught in panic. The sweat on my palms made the attempt to grip the edges of the seat beneath me an exercise in futility. We were going to die.

Tomorrow the police would be knocking at my parents' door to tell them about the wreck. They'd want to know how I knew the guy driving, and my parents wouldn't have a clue how I met him. I was going to die with him, and I didn't even know his name. "Are you sure this is safe?"

"We're not going that fast. Just a bad axle."

I didn't know what he defined as fast, but the needle on the dash pointed closer to a hundred than to eighty. I decided not to argue.

"Almost there."

I didn't know what he was talking about. We weren't almost anywhere. It might have been years since I'd been here, but I still remembered the red, wooden covered bridge we crossed before town.

Franklin let out a low half-growl. He wasn't impressed by the last few minutes' drive. I could feel him clawing at the floor of his carrier through the thick plastic. His eyes flashed in the dimness, and he seemed to be staring at the guy in the driver's seat.

Just as suddenly as I'd driven into it, the fog was gone. We were on the bridge. He'd been right after all.

The town was just in front of us. No one would make a mistake of calling it a sprawling suburb. Only a few hundred people still lived here, most of them descended from the original settlers. Part of me always wondered how many would choose to live here if they'd just rename the town. I mean, who would choose to live in Devil's Vale? It sounded kind of sketchy.

In the distance, I could see Main Street. As cheerful and picturesque as any street I'd ever seen on television, if you didn't look too closely, the heart of Devil's Vale seemed innocuous enough. Cast iron street lights with two luminaries per post stood sentinel the entire length of the street.

I turned and looked over my shoulder, almost as an afterthought. The fog was gone. Part of me wondered if I'd dreamed it. I'd let the trees closing in on me get inside my head. A blanket of fog that thick couldn't simply disappear. No sign of a breeze ruffled the charcoal-colored banners.

Dark windows looked back at me from the bakery in the middle of Main Street.

The only hint that the town hadn't plunged into some type of blackout came from the tiniest shop—one that stood almost directly across from the bakery and next door to Kate's shop. A faint, flickering, golden glow leaked out from behind lace curtains. I peered at the name painted on the window. Scents and Such. I'd have to stop and introduce myself to the only night-owl in town.

"Most everything in town's closed up this time of night. I can drop you at the gas station. You can wait there until someone comes to pick you up." Tall, Dark and Muscular seemed more than a little annoyed with himself for stopping to help.

And here's where I'd go from Damsel in Distress to More than a Little Annoying.

"Actually, I don't have anyone I can call." Mrs. Smith from the lawyer's office might be expecting me, but I could pretty well guarantee that didn't also come with an expectation I'd call her for a ride. "At least not anymore. But if you wouldn't mind dropping me off at my aunt's house, I can probably figure out a way to get my truck in the morning."

"Your aunt lives around here?"

"She did."

"Did?" He flinched. "Sorry. When you asked me to drop you off, I thought she…" He slowed to a stop at the only traffic light in town, and a faint mask of suspicion slid over his face in the glow of the red light. "Who's your aunt?"

"You probably don't know her." Who was I kidding? This was Devil's Vale. Everyone knew everyone. With my luck, this was the local help I was going to be firing tomorrow. "She used to run the antique shop."

"You're Kate's niece?" His not-so-vaguely freaked out vibe was back.

"I was."

He gave a huff, nostrils flaring as he shook his head in a how-did-I-get-into-this-mess kind of way. I could have sworn he cussed under his breath. Then he floored it.

We bumped down two more dirt roads before arriving at the corner of now-dilapidated bricks that once marked the gate at the edge of Kate's property. I didn't need to worry about leaving the keys to the gate in the truck. Judging from the weeds growing up on either side of the gate, it hadn't been shut in a long time.

My friends at school used to joke that the old Victorian was haunted. Their eyes would bulge when I told them I lived in that house. They'd still whisper stories about ghosts—just never around me.

I was never afraid. The house wasn't haunted. I would know.

But I couldn't exactly tell them that.

We pulled into the once-familiar driveway, and he slowed his car without turning off the engine. He turned to look at me in an unmistakable This is Where You Get Out signal. I reached for the handle of the door, realizing for the first time that I'd left my bag back in my truck. This wouldn't be the best time for me to ask him to drive me back.

"Leave me the keys to your truck."

"What?"

"Toss me the keys. Please tell me you brought them with you." His voice held an unearned note of exasperation that faded when I dangled the keys in front of him. "I've got a buddy who can fix anything he sets his hands on. I'll get him to help me with it once it's light out."

"You don't have to do that."

"You got anyone else to help you?"

"No." I hated to admit being helpless. I'd never been helpless in my life.

"Then I'm going to need your keys."

I peeled the key to Kate's house off the ring before placing the rest in his outstretched hand. I hopped out of the seat, bringing Franklin's carrier with me, and paused before closing the door.

"Thanks." I hesitated. "I'm Reese, by the way...I don't even know your name."

"Everyone around here calls me Max."

Chapter Two

ॐ

Colton

I pulled yet another dusty picture frame off the wall and placed it on top of the pile in the cardboard box before I stepped back to study my progress. Not even halfway yet. I rubbed my palms over my eyes with a mixture of fatigue and just general regret that I was even packing up this office. Coach Graves always seemed larger than life. Nothing could take him down. And then to lose him like we did... It made my stomach rumble just like drinking too much water during the first practice in August.

Damn. All the times I'd been in this office, I'd never realized just how much this room was a history of the last few decades in the town's life, at least where football was concerned. I'd been working for hours—hours I hadn't planned to spend alone.

I studied the picture again and winced. I reached for a wad of damp paper towels that I'd already used too many times today and wiped the red-speckled glass. The cleaning crew had missed another spot. Thinking about who planned to be with me today and why we needed to clean out the office in the first place, maybe it was better I was here by myself after all.

I didn't have a clue what Max planned to do with all his dad's pictures. Knowing his current state of mind, he was probably going to burn them. Then he'd regret it next week.

Maybe I should just load all the boxes in the back of my truck and take them with me. With all the crap my parents stuck in the cabin, no one would notice another box.

Another hour or two's work, and I'd finally be done.

Then I could finally get started on Kate's house. She'd been specific about the date she wanted me to get started on repairs—a little too specific, now that I thought about it. She'd written tomorrow's date on the check when she gave it to me.

And then she died. The lady from the bank called me to say that Kate had left them a note saying that I was still supposed to work through her list. And it was a hell of a list. I'd practically be living at the house this summer.

I wished that she'd hired someone else or that I hadn't agreed. If I hadn't agreed to do the work, I could get out of here—disappear, leave the dust of this town behind me...where it belonged.

If my mom could see me right now I'd get a lecture of epic proportions. I scrubbed my face with my palm. What kind of Waters left the house looking less than perfectly groomed?

The kind of Waters who was helping his best friend clean up after his dad's suicide.

Why hadn't anyone seen it coming? Didn't people who were depressed show some kind of signs? Giving important things away? Becoming kind of withdrawn? Coach Graves didn't even call Max to say goodbye.

What the fuck was he thinking that day?

First Kate dropped dead on her porch. Then Coach Graves shot himself in his office. These things ran in threes, didn't they? One Polk. One Graves. Was a Waters next?

14

My heart sped like I'd been running sprints. I knew exactly which one I'd choose. If fate took care of my father for me, I'd give her a high-five.

A metallic squeak almost made me drop the photograph. Damn, for an empty building, this old school had plenty of bumps, thuds, and echoes. I'd gone out into the hall twice just today, looking for whoever's boots were clomping down the hall.

At least this time the light on the alarm panel showed movement at the gym door. Finally. Only one person had a key to the back doors of the school. I tossed another two pictures in the almost full box while I waited for him to arrive.

"Took you long enough." I pointed to the clock on the wall. "I'm pretty sure the words 'on my way' don't typically mean in two hours."

"Had a little delay." Max stood halfway in the door to the office. When the principal called to tell him to empty his dad's office or the janitor was going to do it for him, I'd volunteered to help. But I didn't know that meant I was going to be doing the packing while wondering where in the hell Max was.

I recognized the expression on his face, and it wasn't one that said I'm-sorry-for-making-you-do-this-alone. Nope. He had been preoccupied with something far different than books or yellowed photographs. "Blonde or redhead?"

"Brunette, if you have to know. But it wasn't like that." He shook his head, using his best innocent expression.

I didn't buy it for a second. It was hard to be angry with him, though. He'd spent the first two weeks after our college graduation dealing with a police investigation, planning a funeral, attending the funeral, and then messing with financial stuff that required a lawyer.

15

Being an only child must suck.

Still, I couldn't let him off too easy. "Sure it wasn't."

"Really." He held up his hands like he wanted to surrender. "I was driving in from picking up more boxes like you said we needed. I took a wrong turn."

"Stop right there." I held my hand up, shooting him a glare. "You took a wrong turn? In Devil's Vale?"

"Not exactly in Devil's Vale. Right outside town." Max shrugged and shook his head in distaste. "I know. I must not have been paying attention. Lucky I did, though. I ran into a girl having car trouble and had to drive her into town."

"You had to, huh?"

"What was I supposed to do? Leave her stranded out by the bridge?"

He had a point. No one deserved to be stranded out there. Not at night. "You didn't tell me that's where she was. What were you doing out there?"

"No idea. Like I said. I got confused. Ended up out on 20. When I came back, there she was." He ran his fingers through his shaggy, black hair. In the past, he'd always kept his hair almost military-short, and I couldn't get used to seeing him like this. His hair was just another sign of all the things that had gone wrong since the last week of May. I didn't think he'd gotten a haircut since before his dad's funeral, and he'd needed one back then. "Sorry. I shouldn't have left you with all this mess."

Come to think of it, I wasn't sure if he'd been in the office since the day the police had called him. I couldn't say that I really blamed him for avoiding it. Even after I'd already boxed almost all his dad's knick-knacks, awards, and old textbooks, the newly painted wall and the new tiles on the ceiling made the memory of what happened in this room too fresh, even for me.

Green eyes just a little too wide, Max toed the threshold like he'd spontaneously combust if he entered the room. That did it. We weren't staying here any longer. I folded the panels of the box closed and ran a strip of packing tape over them. "Tell you what. I've been here long enough. Why don't we call it a day?"

"No, I can do this," he protested. But his expression said he couldn't.

"Look." I gestured around the room. Almost everything left was property of Devil's Vale Independent School District. "We can come back in the morning and finish up in an hour. If I pack any more tonight, I'm going to turn into a box myself."

I didn't need to say that the old, empty building crossed my creeped-out tolerance an hour ago. I'd only stayed because he wasn't answering his cell phone, and I wanted to make sure he didn't try to tackle this himself. Spend enough time in here alone, and anyone would start seeing ghosts.

"I don't care what they do with the rest of this shit." Max's voice rose with the same annoyed edge that it always got when he'd had a pass picked off in an interception.

He was in over his head, and he didn't have anyone else to help him. Well, he didn't have anyone who wasn't a member of the not-quite-dead-yet Sunday school class at his dad's church to help. He didn't need their whispers making this any harder. That's why I was helping my teammate when he was in trouble.

"I don't have anything better to do. You know that."

"Too well. When are you going to talk with your dad about your little issue?" Max hit upon the topic I'd been trying to avoid.

My little issue. He'd graced my situation with the nickname to make it seem less important than it was. As I'd driven down the roads leading from campus to home, I'd barely been able to think of anything else. I'd stayed behind, waiting to hear word from my interview. I should have known it wasn't going to be good news. When the medical school spread good news, it didn't wait to call you last.

We'd been dancing around my issue for close to a month. Dealing with the loss of Max's dad had almost made things easier. Almost. No one expected to get the call from the principal yesterday announcing that he had to clear out the office by Sunday, least of all him. He was also the least prepared to deal with cleaning up the aftermath of the end of his only parent.

"Honestly, no idea. I've been waiting for him to be in a good mood."

"With your dad, you're going to be waiting a while."

"I know." I brushed my hands on my jeans. I tucked the worn, leather chair into its familiar home at the oversized desk before heading toward the door. "I have one thing my sister needs me to do, but give me an hour and meet me at my place."

"You're Shelby's errand-boy now?"

"She had to stay late tonight, making sure she was set up for the festival. And besides, she saw a letter from Augusta."

"Ah, so she's blackmailing you. That one's impressive."

I didn't need to see that glint in Max's eye. I'd seen it plenty of times when we were partying at a sorority house. The last thing any of us needed was Max turning his bad-boy vibe on Shelby.

"Just bring the beer." The discussion was over.

"Your mom will kill you if she finds us drinking."

"My mom never wanders down to the cabin. Not unless it's daylight."

He didn't pretend like he wasn't relieved we were heading out of the office. For a while we just walked, and I let myself relax with every step we took.

But I could sense a question hanging in the air. As we passed the humming water fountains, he finally gave up and asked it. "Do you think your dad's going to let you stay here?"

"Mom'll probably make him. At least for now. He's probably going to want me to come to work on the ranch."

"You're going to love that."

I let out a long breath. "Yeah. Not exactly what I had planned."

"You. On the ranch. That's...that's kind of funny."

"Sure it is. It's freakin' hilarious. Dad's going to be thrilled to trap me in the business. He didn't want me to go to med school in the first place." A lifetime of smelling like horses. Exactly what I'd always wanted. Exactly why I'd tried to escape.

Max laughed for the first time in weeks. I didn't even have to look at him to know he was shaking his head, but I did. Sure enough, he had his best you-have-to-be-fuckin'-kidding-me expression on his face while he ran his fingers through his hair as if someone had dumped a cup of spiders on top of him.

We'd been friends since before either of us could pronounce the word friend. I didn't remember a time that he wasn't seated at our family's table for Sunday dinner. We could finish each other's sentences, but there were things that even Max didn't understand. Things I wasn't allowed to explain.

"That's going to go well."

"Tell me about it. I'm not sure if I really have a choice." With student loans already begging to be repaid and parents who'd given the We're Not Paying for Your College lecture not quite four years ago, I never really imagined myself in this scenario.

High school valedictorian. Captain of the football team. Member of the right fraternity. Getting into my choice of med schools should have been a breeze.

Should have.

Seems like I had a whole lot of should-haves lately.

"So you're just staying here?"

Being a Waters in this town carries a responsibility. Even without my dad in the room, I could hear his voice echoing in my head. "Until I figure something else out, yeah, I'm staying here. I don't really have much other choice."

"Sure you do." He shrugged, and his collar pulled back just enough to reveal the crow tattoo he'd recently gotten. "There's always a choice."

"Speaking of choices, you're still taking that job in Seattle?"

"Money's great." Max pursed his lips and nodded like a dashboard bobble head. "It's a great job. I can't turn it down."

He sounded like he wanted me to believe he was excited, but something in his voice was forced. He *needed* me to believe he wanted to take this job, even though he'd never mentioned applying for it. One day he was the last one standing next to the freshly covered grave in Devil's Vale's cemetery, and the next he'd taken a job out of state.

"You ever going to tell me what it is?"

"If I told you, I'd have to kill you."

I waited for him to laugh, but it didn't come. "Never really figured you for one of those kind of jobs."

He swallowed, and a hard edge came into his voice. "Maybe you don't know me as well as you think you do."

Was that why couldn't he look me in the eyes?

"You know, you don't have to go. Hell, you can stay with me." I pushed open the heavy doors leading to the locker rooms. Our footsteps echoed through the empty, tiled hallway. I was surprised to realize I was happy not to be alone. The place was filled with spirits of football players past. Even in the dead of summer, the locker rooms never lost their odor of sweat, grass, mud, and teenage hormones gone wild.

"Look, there's nothing here for me. Except for you, of course. But bro, I just don't roll that way." Max half laughed and shoved his hands in the pockets of his jacket. It shouldn't have been cold enough for jackets. Not in June. Not in Georgia.

"You don't know how lucky you are to be getting out of here."

"Trust me, Colton, I do." He hit the crash bar to the door leading outside. He took a deep breath, and I could almost see the relief spreading across his face. I hadn't realized how badly he wanted to move, to leave Devil's Vale and its memories behind. Max had always been a guy of few words. Since he'd taken the job in Seattle, he'd become a man of even fewer.

We descended the steps without talking. We'd been down this path more times than I could count: pee wee football players leaving high school camp; middle school teammates when our school's field was damaged after a wave of vandalism hit the town; finally, championship co-quarterbacks from the first team to win state. Everyone predicted the guys from our team were destined to do great things.

Destiny was a funny thing.

Chapter Three

Temporary home. Just for a few weeks. A month tops. It would be a great experience for me. I might even be able to talk my professors into giving me some extra credit. After all, the master's program had an independent study component. This was about to be a hell of a lot of solo work. Even mostly hidden by darkness, I could tell this house was only fit to be a temporary home to rats, mice, and maybe cockroaches.

I'd worked on a lot of renovations. This one was a teardown if I'd ever seen one. And I was stuck here alone. A string of profanities that would have earned a mouthful of soap from my mom stopped just short of coming out.

Just turned 22 or not, my mom raised me to be a Polk, a Southern lady. And true Southern ladies didn't cuss. She obviously didn't spend nearly enough time in the anthropology department at the University of Galveston—either that or I spent far too much.

Even though the only illumination came from the glow of the moon filtering through the thick grove of pine trees, I could easily make out just how badly the house had fallen into disrepair. How had this place not been condemned?

I stood at the foot of the steps, still tasting dust the wheels of the sports car kicked up as it peeled away from me. That guy, Max, took off with a speed that suggested his wife was delivering a baby somewhere.

Franklin hissed with impatience. I wasn't sure if he sensed we weren't moving anymore or if he was just picking up on my freaked-out vibe.

It didn't matter either way since we were here.

And I *was* freaked out. Sure, I'd been nervous when my parents had informed me I was about to do my first solo job of clearing out an estate, but I'd been working with them since I was old enough to pack boxes. When a family couldn't sift through a relative's belongings, they called in the experts. We could tell what was sentimental, what was trash, and what might have some value.

It didn't pay particularly well, but it was a great cover for what we really did for a living. And that was something else a proper Southern lady didn't discuss in polite conversation.

Sifting through the Polk House should have been a breeze, since Kate owned an antiques shop. She should have been the most skilled at preservation of all of us. But even from the darkened front yard, I could tell this wasn't the house I remembered or the one my mom fondly described to me. Back when we drove away from Devil's Vale for what was supposed to be the last time, the estate was the pride and joy of the family.

Now?

Well, it was probably better that my mom wasn't here to see this. For the first time, I considered the car accident a mixed blessing. Mom wouldn't have been able to stand seeing, well...what was still standing.

The cupola was still there. I couldn't tell if the tin still glistened so brightly it threatened to blind anyone in a three-mile radius, though. Probably not. It seemed different somehow, almost askew. I desperately hoped that was just a trick of the moonlight. If the roof had shifted, I was probably going to be dealing with a leak on top of everything else. I hated mold.

The cast-iron weathervane was still there, but the horse hung at a sad angle. I wasn't sure if Prancer could even spin any longer. I doubted it. Studying the rest of the exterior of the house was probably better left until morning. Or better yet, until after a few stiff drinks.

Now I understood why my dad met me at my truck before I headed out. He'd given me a what-your-mom-doesn't-know-won't-hurt-her look and handed me a cooler loaded with an assortment of my preferred hard cider. I was underage, and this city was dry—as in, no alcohol was sold in town. When he handed me the cooler, he gave me a grave nod like I was about to drive into some version of *Footloose*.

"Come on, Franklin." Clutching the cat carrier like it was a shield, I worked up enough courage to approach the porch. The house was beyond dark.

It looked dead. Empty. An unwelcome shudder rippled up my spine.

If the moon hadn't been full, I wouldn't have even been able to see the stairs to the porch that meandered its way around the entire house. Since half of them were split or rotting away, giving dim view to the hollow below them, I needed all the light I could get. The floorboards creaked suspiciously beneath my feet like they were trying to warn me. I didn't belong here.

You shouldn't be here. The thought pressed down on me as if someone was whispering into my ear. *You should leave.*

It took me two attempts to swallow. I'd never let a house scare me before, no matter its reputation, no matter who or what might still live there. I was born to do this. The fatigue from the drive was messing with my head. That was it. I was just tired. All I needed was a decent night's sleep. I pushed away thoughts of the almost-voice.

I had the right to be here.

Maybe it would look better in the daylight. I stifled a laugh. One thing I'd learned years ago, no restoration project looked better in the clarity of bright light.

I crossed the porch, praying that the boards would hold my weight. I'd never considered myself big. I'd always been small for my age, always on the front row of group pictures, but I wondered if I'd be better off if I could fly right now. Something skittered in the space under the porch. I didn't want to meet whatever made the noise.

Not even the doorbell was lit. When I called to make arrangements to begin the process of cleaning the house out, the lawyer's secretary promised that she'd paid the electric bill. If she'd lied to me, I would be spending the night at her house tonight. That is, if I could figure out a way to get over there.

I dug in my pocket for the key. My mom had always kept it carefully wrapped in a lace handkerchief. She was determined that someday she'd be able to go home. My dad disagreed. And that was my cue to leave the room.

The doorknob turned with surprising ease. At least something was in decent shape around here. If the outside was a bit dark, inside the house was a black hole. The darkness was so thick and complete, it was almost alive. At any moment, it would reach out and pull me in.

I swung Franklin's crate out in front of me to ward off...well, I didn't know what I was warding off, but it gave me the courage to cross the threshold. I skimmed my hand up the wall, feeling where a light switch should be.

No dice.

Of course, this house had been built back before they kept decent records and far before they even thought about things like the proper placement of electrical plugs and light switches. I just needed to look a little harder.

As I ran my hand up the fuzzy wallpaper, I desperately hoped that the texture beneath my fingers was part of the design and not spider webs or something worse. I'd seen almost everything while I was at school. We'd been called in to salvage more than one house where an elderly relative had died.

I just didn't want to live in one of those houses. Those houses were for someone else. Not my cup of tea.

My fingers found the switch just as my right calf found something else. Hard, pointy, and refusing to budge, the box was just below my knee, and it took every ounce of yoga I'd practiced to keep myself on two feet. I blindly slapped at the wall and froze.

Disaster didn't even begin to halfway describe it.

The outside of the house was model-home ready in comparison with the inside.

I was well aware that Aunt Kate was technically Great-Aunt Kate, and I knew she'd been far closer to a hundred than she'd been to fifty. But still.

The box that introduced itself to my knee wasn't alone. From one side of the foyer to the other, boxes, crates, and trash bags full of stuff I probably didn't want to know about were stacked in columns from the floor almost completely to the ceiling.

Kate was a hoarder.

Somewhere along the way, she'd changed from expert collector to someone who couldn't dare to throw anything away. Wadded newsprint, empty tissue boxes, crates of broken toys, and boxes of old plates were piled precariously atop each other.

Collecting and selling antiques worked in tandem with the family business. At least the business we admitted to in polite conversation. We all knew that proper preservation was the key element between a valuable item and just a piece of trash.

So how had Kate allowed this to happen?

Something scratched at the door, and I halfway expected to discover the team from the show about the hoarders descending. And I wouldn't tell them to leave. My mom expected me to get this place ready to sell before school started.

No problem. As long as I wanted to take an entire year off.

Crap. I backed against the wall and slid to the floor in defeat. How had I gotten into this?

I could almost hear my mom's voice when she called to discuss the issue with me. "Now, Reese, you owe it to the family."

You'd think we were part of the mafia or some secret society. At home, it was *the family* this and *the family* that, and we had to do it for *the family's* sake. People in New Orleans didn't even know who the Polks were.

I wasn't even a real Polk. My last name was Everett— just like my dad. But I still couldn't shake the whole family business thing. Outside of Devil's Vale, we were just normal.

As normal as a family could be when they also operated a ghost tour company, but everyone assumed Ghosts of

Bourbon Street was just for fun. Tourists came to New Orleans for a good time.

Everyone knew the stories: vampires, voodoo, witches, ghosts.

Our reservations booked months in advance. We helped tourists have a good time—fun and games, scary stories to give goosebumps in the night.

Or at least that's what we told everyone. Our ghost tour company had amazingly accurate stories. Not every company had a legitimate seer. But none of our customers needed to know about that. They didn't need to know about me.

I was the family secret, and it needed to stay that way.

Franklin's hiss had changed from mildly annoyed to about to pee in this cat carrier just because he was ticked off at me. He'd do it too.

My eyes burned. There must be a ton of mold in here. Definitely a roof leak. I took one more look around the living room. And that was a surprise to me?

"Just a second." I peeked into the carrier, speaking more sharply than I'd planned. This wasn't his fault. Annoyed green eyes glared back at me. "Damn. Your litter box was in the back of the truck. You're going to have to punt tonight. Maybe Kate has something we can use around here."

I rocked onto my knees and stood with difficulty, afraid that one wrong move would bury me. I bumped my shoulder against a cardboard version of the Leaning Tower of Pisa. And then I'd have to find a room where I was certain I could let Franklin out without risking him getting squished, lost, or eaten by anything alive in here.

Ordinarily I would have left him at home. He wasn't a bad traveler; he was a horrible one. Cat carriers just weren't his thing. In his opinion, he belonged on the windowsill plotting ways to get through the glass to capture the hummingbirds around their feeders. When he was unhappy, he made sure I knew it. Loudly. So I left him at home.

Not this trip. This time Mom insisted. She squished him into her carrier herself, not a small feat when she had a cast up to her hip.

"The only thing we have to fear is fear itself." The quote was intended to reassure a panicked public. Franklin's presence was intended to keep me calm. After seeing the condition of Kate's house, I thought that maybe we had more than one thing to fear. Dying by suffocation from a landslide of stuff was high on my list right now.

My phone vibrated in my pocket. Right now was not the time for me to have a conversation with my mother. If she had any idea Kate's house looked like this, I needed a warning...or permission to just burn the place.

I pressed the red decline button with equal relief and satisfaction. But since I didn't want to give my mother a stroke and I couldn't handle two dead relatives right now...I quickly keyed in a message.

I'm here. I'm fine. You are seriously going to owe me.

Before I added anything else I'd regret later, I powered my phone off. My mom had the memory of an elephant, and she wasn't afraid to use it like a weapon.

I picked my way through what could almost be considered a path through the piles of junk until I was standing more or less in the once-formal den. Stacks of cardboard reached almost to the ceiling. If Aunt Kate hadn't been an antiques collector with a once-great eye for things of value, I'd call a junk collector to just haul everything out of here so I could leave this death trap before it added me to its list of victims.

Even Dr. Savage wouldn't be prepared for a house like this. As head of the modern anthropology department, he'd probably have a heart attack if I sent him a picture of the house. If he weren't in Ireland, I'd call him to see if he had a team of grad students who'd like to get some extra credit. Digging through Kate's stuff could probably get them an entire semester of hands-on experience.

If I let Franklin out in here, I might never find him again. I turned around and started to make my way down the foot-wide pathway leading to the hallway that would eventually take me to the staircase. Maybe the junk situation was confined to the front rooms of the house.

I was almost lucky. The further I got down the hallway, the more room I had to maneuver. It only took one giant step to clear a wooden crate and arrive in a room that was basically empty except for a desk and a couch. By then, I was as relieved as my cat was about to be.

"Good luck, buddy." I opened the door, expecting Franklin to bolt like a rocket out of his crate. But he stayed put. His eyes seemed to be studying what must have been Kate's office. His eyes darted to the corners of the room, and he hissed as if he were challenging a larger cat trying to venture into his turf.

"Ok, Frank, do what you want." I stood and walked out of the room, closing the door behind me. I didn't need his help to make me feel nervous about being here.

Tea. I could use a cup of tea. Aunt Kate was who introduced me to the nerve-settling quality of good English tea in the first place. Surely she'd still have some in the kitchen.

Oh God, the kitchen.

Dealing with a kitchen at a hoarder's house was normally a lesson in nausea. And that was when I could throw remains of things I'd rather not examine too closely in a dumpster, go home, take a shower, and brew myself a cup of tea. Now the hoarder's kitchen was my kitchen.

Maybe it wouldn't be too bad.

And Franklin might really be a purple dinosaur in disguise.

I closed my eyes and tried to remember how to get to the kitchen through what would best be described as a maze. I crossed the dining room. Peeking down, I could see the mahogany legs of the dining room table buried under what looked like piles of magazines and newspaper. No lit candles allowed in this room.

And I went through the parlor. The ivory lace curtains over the bay windows let in a hint of moonlight, revealing far more overstuffed trash bags than I hoped to see.

I found the kitchen without as much trouble as I'd thought. I stood in the doorway, closing my eyes and taking a deep breath to prepare me for what was coming next. Then I looked around.

The kitchen looked like a kitchen. Oddly enough, it even smelled vaguely lemony, thanks to a plug-in air freshener on the wall. Thankfully, it was even stuff-free.

What was going on? I'd never seen a house like this. Hoarding tendencies didn't just stop at the kitchen doorway.

But then I remembered one of Kate's favorite bits of wisdom. Antiques and grease don't mix—whether she was discussing grease from a kitchen, dripping wax from a candle, or grime from someone's fingers, she'd always been beyond careful about proper preservation, which is what weirded me out about the house.

It shouldn't be this way.

She was one of the first people to introduce me to the world of the proper care of delicate things. Knick-knacks that others might toss could find a home at her store. The way she told the story as to why she selected each item made customers eager to take whatever they'd been looking at home with them—no matter what it might be. Few people really needed a set of ancient hair curlers, but even fewer could resist Aunt Kate.

I stepped fully into the kitchen, too tired to understand the vast difference in the state of the kitchen from the rest of the house. For now, I was just going to settle for being relieved that the kitchen seemed to be a safe place in the house.

Looking around the kitchen, I was convinced I wasn't the first person to enter the house since Kate had passed away. The kitchen should have been filled with the stomach-churning odor of spoiled food gone to waste, but it almost smelled like disinfectant.

Thankfully, the kitchen caretaker had emptied the refrigerator but didn't take her tea. Two boxes of her favorite stood on the bottom shelf of the cabinet. The second one was still in its clear, plastic wrapper. I picked that one, and I tossed the open one into the trash. Just because Kate had done a fair job of keeping her vintage goods protected didn't mean that care went into food storage. I reached back into the cabinet and took out a mug.

That's when the noises outside changed. The chickens weren't just cooing like they had been just minutes earlier; they were cackling. Honestly, if chickens could scream, they were. Something was outside. My stomach lurched, and I looked out into the woods bordering the house. Who knew what kinds of things lived out there?

Things that probably liked the taste of chicken.

I wasn't going to stand here and let them die—even if I wasn't sure where they were. I looked around for something to beat off wild dogs or foxes or bears. Were there bears in Georgia?

Part of me really wanted to stay in the kitchen, but I knew that I'd just be stuck wondering what was outside. I picked up the rolling pin—sure, that was going to help—stepped out of the kitchen toward the back door, and paused in front of the fireplace. That cast-iron ash shovel looked much sturdier than the rolling pin. I tossed the wooden pin down in exchange for the deadlier weapon.

I swallowed—twice—and gripped the doorknob, ignoring how badly my hands shook. It was probably just a dog or maybe a stray cat. Something that roamed the woods in the middle of the night.

The door creaked like it hadn't been opened for a while. I had to tug it to convince it to open. Just as I took a step outside, I heard the distinct crunch of boots on dried grass. Not a cat. Not a dog. A definite someone.

"Who's out here?"

Only silence answered. Yes, Reese, because a wolf's going to happily answer you.

Silence and chickens. Really loud chickens. I followed their cackles and froze.

Someone was standing there. Dark t-shirt. Dark jeans. He fit the exact description of someone who was up to no good—selecting a lonely house basically in the middle of nowhere. The owner had just died. No one should be home. Easy pickings.

I did not sign up for this. "What are you doing here?"

Absolutely no response. God, this guy was confident. And now he was walking toward the house. I stepped as close to the guy as I dared, put the shovel on my shoulder, and swung.

Chapter Four
☙☙

Colton

My head was freezing. And in pain. The way my eyes were watering, it felt like the time I'd played not-quite-touch football and Chris Nelson had gotten a little too into the game. Damn his head was hard. His team had taken home the first place trophy, and I'd won a trip to the emergency room and a lecture from my dad about the fact that, even though I was twelve, I was smart enough to know better.

I hadn't played football without my helmet since then. So why did my head hurt so bad? Why was it cold?

And it smelled weird. Old-people weird. Aunt Tilly's house smelled like this. Mold. Mothballs. Like when I followed Shelby into the antique shop next to her store.

But I wasn't shopping with my sister. So what the hell was going on?

I cracked my eyes open. At first I only saw a blur. And boxes. A completely black cat sat on my chest, flicking its tail back and forth like I was a mouse and it was starving.

A little girl I didn't know stood facing the fireplace, chewing on her thumbnail. I studied her a little longer. She was curvy. Very curvy, in fact. Too curvy to be a little girl, but she was really short. As my vision cleared, I could see her profile better. Not a teenager either. Probably not much older than twenty.

I gingerly reached up to examine my too-cold head and felt a plastic bag of... peas? I tried to sit up, but the cat refused to budge. It blinked at me as if it was telling me it knew what was best.

It growled.

"Shh, Franklin. Don't wake him up. I'm still trying to figure out what to do. Oh crap!"

Mystery girl noticed I was awake. Her face was pale as a sheet, chocolate-brown hair curled over one shoulder. The darkest brown eyes I'd ever seen were tinged with guilt and worry.

"Oh my gosh. I'm so sorry. I just... I didn't..." Words tripped over each other in what I thought was probably an attempt at an apology. "The chickens... They were screaming. I've never heard chickens before. At least not like that. My parents don't have any chickens, just Kate. Well, she did. And it was dark. And you looked like a bad guy."

The events of the night started to fall back into place. I'd left the school, promising Max he could come over for a few beers before he flew out, but first I had to stop and feed Kate's damn chickens. I'd just finished refilling the feed bowls when something hit me from behind.

"You thought I was a bad guy?" Did anyone over the age of ten even use that phrase?

I sat up on one elbow and started to laugh. Insanely bad idea. The room blurred, and stars swam at the corners of my eyes.

"I'm so sorry." She knelt next to the loveseat, biting her lip. "In my defense, though, I did give you a chance to say who you were." She reached for a cord dangling from my pocket. "I just didn't realize you were wearing earbuds. At least not until it was too late. Sorry."

37

"You hit me." I was surprised I could form words. From the look on her face, so was she. "Damn, you can swing."

"My dad once wanted a son. He played baseball in college and made sure I knew how to bat. I was always the first one picked for a team." Her words tumbled over each other like they were running around the bases in a tied game.

"I can see why. If Devil's Vale ever gets a rec team, you should play." I was trying to make her feel better, but it wasn't working.

Why was I trying to make her feel better? She was the one who'd hit me.

Now that she was closer, I could see her better. She wasn't as young as I'd thought she was at first. If I had to guess, she was probably twenty-two or twenty-three, not more than twenty-five. Her face seemed young, but the stress in her eyes told a different story.

Her hand curled into a fist, and she pressed it against her lips. A tear started to form in her eyes. She was not going to start crying on me. Just...no.

"It was an accident." Her voice was pleading for me to believe her.

"You accidentally hit me with a bat."

She shook her head. "Not a bat." She nodded toward a miniature shovel leaning against Kate's old desk. "I think it's to scoop ashes out of a fireplace."

"That thing's cast iron. How the hell did you swing that?"

"I'm stronger than I look."

"I can tell." I reached up to touch my head, but she caught my hand.

"I wouldn't." She bit her damn lip again. It must be the head wound because that had to be one of the sexiest things I'd ever seen. "There's no blood, just a lump."

That was a relief. And then I remembered something. I'd been outside. As far as I could tell, she was alone. "How'd I get in here?"

"Like I said, I'm stronger than I look." She glanced down at my pants. "I kind of dragged you. You're going to need to wash those jeans."

"And what exactly made you decide I wasn't here to break in?"

"When you fell, I saw the chicken feed. I figured you weren't here for petty theft."

I nodded. Another horrible idea.

Observant, smart...two things not typically found in girls from this town. "Where'd you come from?"

"Louisiana. I'm Kate's niece...well, great niece. I came to clear this place out."

"Wait a minute. When Mrs. Smith called, she said someone was coming, but you don't exactly fit the description of who she told me to watch for." She was definitely not a woman in her mid-forties who was a dead ringer for Kate in her younger years.

"My mom was supposed to be the one to do this, but she was in a car accident last week. She broke her leg in two places and can't even get off the couch."

"That makes two of us." I tried to laugh, but each laugh was punctuated by a reminder of exactly how fast my heart was beating, courtesy of the pain in my temples.

"I'm so sorry." She rocked back on her heels and sat cross-legged on the floor. "I've been jumpy since I got here."

She shot a look like knives being thrown at the cat. It wisely jumped down and retreated to the top of a bookshelf. "He isn't helping."

I reached up and grabbed the makeshift ice pack. "You know, this isn't such a bad idea."

"I've had a lot of experience with bumps and bruises." She tried to smile, but worry still won out. "I should probably take you somewhere to get that checked out."

Her hand almost reached out and touched my forehead. I tried not to notice how much her fingers were shaking.

"Nah." I sat up slowly. Now that the cat was removed from my chest, breathing came much more easily. "I'll be fine." I sat up slowly. Nothing blurred this time, and only two stars swam at the edge of my vision.

"Well, I still don't think you should drive. Want me to take you somewhere? Do you have someone I can call?"

"No, I'm really ok." I stood. The floor stayed where it was supposed to be, and none of the lights changed colors. "I think I'll be heading home now."

∂ဌ

"So she was a real knockout?" Max tossed the can of beer in my direction with a smile that was desperately trying to not turn into a laugh.

"Don't even start." I cautiously held the unopened can against the ostrich egg- sized lump on the side of my head. When she'd said she could swing, she wasn't kidding. "Why didn't you tell me there was someone at Kate's house?"

"You just said you had to do something. You didn't tell me where. I didn't know you were feeding the chickens."

"Blame Shelby for that one. She said we couldn't let the chickens starve. I've gone over there every night since Kate died."

"So that's where you've been disappearing to. I thought you were keeping a girl on the down-low."

"Like that would ever happen."

"You never know." He shrugged innocently. "Should we blame Shel for your concussion too?" Max leaned back and kicked his feet onto the wicker basket currently pretending to be my coffee table.

I tried to ignore the fact that he had a nickname for my sister.

Instead, I focused on the fact that I might be staying here for a while and most of my furniture was still back in Augusta. I figured showing up with a trailer full of furniture would only announce my plans had changed. To be honest, none of the stuff was worth anything. I might even leave it at the apartment. Max tried to look like he was comfortable in a chair that even most resale shops would have refused.

At some point in the past, this cabin would have been the overseer's house. My mom had once used it for storage. My dad used it to hold stuff he didn't want to look at any longer—including me.

He hadn't exactly planned on me being here for the summer.

Neither had I.

I had yet to figure out why the medical school in Augusta had suddenly decided I was no longer the right candidate for them. I'd met the professors and taken the tour, even put a nonrefundable deposit down on a condo walking distance from campus. I'd been in. Then I wasn't.

Staying in Devil's Vale had never been included on any of my ideas for a perfect future. And yet, here I was.

As much as I hated to admit it, the unexpected mess with Max's dad had been a good distraction when I got here. Obviously, I had to stay and help my best friend sort out the mess that was left of his life. But now Max was leaving. And so was my excuse to stay here.

I was going to have to admit the reason I wasn't leaving.

As much as he talked about family, commitment, and honor, Dad was happier while I was out of state. I was happier too. We communicated best from a two-hour plane's flight away. I'd even wondered if Augusta was going to be too close to home, and now I was stuck here.

Max snapped his fingers a half inch from my nose. "Dude, you sure you don't want me to take you up to Atlanta and get that looked at? I've been talking to you for five minutes."

"No. I'm fine."

"You look fine." His laugh won, and he dissolved into a fit of laughter reminiscent of nights he'd spent at my house after the team had finished celebrating our victory on the field.

"How much did you have to drink?"

"Not nearly enough for that story." Max fought for control as he gulped down half his beer. "And you never even got Mystery Girl's name either?"

"Somehow I didn't think to ask. Waking up unconscious inside Kate's house kind of threw me for a loop."

"Sounds fair." He inclined his beer in my direction, conceding the point, and squinted one eye closed, studying my face like a detective looking at a crime scene. "Tell me what she looks like again."

"You saw her."

"But it was dark. And I was in a hurry. I didn't have time to focus."

"Focus. Right. You're just trying to decide if you want to hit on her before you leave."

"Just tell me what she looked like." A hint of a smile played at the corner of his lips. He thought something was funny, and I didn't have a clue what it was.

"All right." I decided to humor him. "Dark brown hair. Brown eyes."

"What kind of brown?"

"Melted chocolate." I flinched. I'd spent too much time in art classes lately.

"How's her body?"

I shot my eyebrows up at him in reply.

"Smokin' hot body." He answered for me.

"I didn't say she was smoking."

Max shook his head. "Colton, my friend, how long have we known each other?"

"Since diapers."

"Exactly. And the only time you haven't gone into explicit detail about a member of the opposite sex's physique is when she's so hot you don't want anyone else to have a chance with her."

I thought about it—the girl from chemistry, the physical therapist in Kansas, my roommate's little sister. Check, check, and check.

He nodded in conceited agreement. "So what are you going to say when you see her again?"

"Who said I was going to see her at all?"

"Didn't Kate already pay you to work on her house?"

Shit. That girl must have hit me harder than I thought. Either that or I was just trying to block it out of my mind. "I'll get Bud down on Oak Street to do it. He could use some extra work."

"Bud's gotten so old he's lucky to be able to find his shop in the mornings. Now, didn't she say she was staying in town until she gets Kate's house ready to sell?"

"Yeah."

"Well, then, Miss Smokin' Hot Mystery Lady's going to need some help—help that Kate already paid you to do."

The clock struck eleven. Max reluctantly got to his feet. "I'd better go. Still have some stuff to do before my flight."

I followed him out the front door, ducking to dodge the moths circling the coach light. The silence grew thicker with each step. For the first time I could remember, I didn't know when I'd see him again.

"Offer's still open." We'd reached Max's car. I could barely see the words "For Sale" shoe-polished on the back window. Damn, I thought Max was going to be buried in that car. "I've got room. You could stay here with me."

"I wish I could, Colt, but it's just not that simple." He flinched like he'd said too much. "You're not the only one who doesn't have a choice." Something had changed in Max's face. He'd aged years in the last few weeks.

We were born exactly one week and one day apart. We were almost twins...well, except for the way we looked. Max was tall and wiry. He had a good five inches on me, and he put that height and slight build to work out on the field, slipping through holes in the defense that would have left me solidly on the ground. Whenever we were in a group, I could always find his mess of raven-black hair sticking up above the rest of the crowd. And I'd be right beside him, looking nothing like his twin. Blond hair. Blue eyes. If we met a girl, one of us would be her type. Normally him.

We'd done everything together, even rooming together in college.

Until now.

Tomorrow morning, everything would change. I convinced myself that was the reason for the change in Max, the wary look in his eyes, the why behind the words I could tell were about to be left unspoken.

"You're coming back to visit, aren't you? You've never missed homecoming in your life."

His only answer was the furrowing of his brow. I didn't miss the fact that he was staring into the lengthening shadows pointing toward the main house.

"Tell you what. I'll buy your car." My words felt strangely final.

"You'll what?" Max looked at me like I'd suddenly sprouted a second head.

"Your car." I ran my hand over the onyx paint. He'd spent more time restoring the once-clunker than he did practicing on the football field, something our coach reminded him with annoying regularity. "I'll buy your car, and then you can have it when you decide to move back."

"I'm not coming back."

I laughed again. I'd said that before. I distinctly remembered standing on my parents' front porch, yelling the exact same words into my dad's reddening face. While my words had been hot with anger, Max's were laced with sadness. "Devil's Vale is like a black hole. You always come back."

"Not me."

"Famous last words." I pulled out my wallet and began thumbing through the last of my remaining cash.

Chapter Five

❦

Reese

The best thing I could say about my first night in Devil's Vale was that it was over. Between welcoming my still-unnamed neighbor with a cast-iron shovel and managing to knock over one of the pillars of boxes, barely missing Franklin in the process, the evening was going on record as one of the top five worst nights I'd experienced. Despite the creaks, snaps, and settling-old-house noises, I'd finally gotten to sleep around three. Two hours later, the chickens had decided that sleeping in wasn't their forte. Finding someone to take the chickens was high on my to-do list.

Civilized people weren't dressed and ready to meet the day by seven on a Saturday morning—at least they weren't back home. My mother never said I was civilized.

I slid my favorite t-shirt over my head and tried to decide between jeans and shorts. If I hadn't carried a change of clothes in my backpack, I'd be stuck wearing the same outfit as yesterday. I made a mental note to send Dr. Savage a thank you note. Some of his methods seemed a little OCD, but today they were proving worthwhile. He wouldn't be cool with the idea that I might be considering working while wearing shorts, but being cool was the whole idea. Still, the anthropology student in me shouted out a reminder to wear jeans while the trickle of sweat meandering down the back of my neck was screaming out a vote for shorts.

Last night was freezing, but the weather today seemed to be prepping for a baptism in a furnace. A visit to Daze Gone By couldn't be too laden with risks. Shorts won the vote.

I buckled my shorts closed and took a moment to study my reflection in the mirror. Between the ponytail curling over my shoulder and the lack of makeup since that wasn't in my emergency backpack, I'd probably be laughed right out of a bar—even one on Bourbon Street. Not that I hadn't already had that happen more than once, enough times really that I'd taken to just carrying my ID before I went on a bar crawl with the rest of the soon-to-be grad students.

A bar crawl sounded really good right now, definitely preferable to exploring the business side of the antique store. Relics, antiques, stories of an item's tawdry past—those I could handle. To be honest, I loved imagining just who might have owned something before it found its way into Kate's collection at Daze Gone By. If just sifting through inventory was all I needed to do, I wouldn't have even hesitated at taking today's to-do list by storm. But a shop meant inventory. And inventory meant bookkeeping. And bookkeeping meant math.

And math was one of the reasons I was an anthropology major.

No need to stall any longer. The faster I could finish off the estate, the faster I could get home. I needed to get to town, and to do that, I needed my truck. My truck with all my supplies, all my clothes...and Franklin's litter box. This morning, I wasn't even sure if I remembered where I'd left it. Everything about my truck stalling and getting stuck in the Fog from Hell seemed more like a dream than reality.

It couldn't be more than three miles into town. I could walk. We easily covered that much ground every Friday and Saturday night. At least that's what the note on the ghost tour website said.

I gave Franklin a parting scratch on the head as he lay sprawled in the center of the bed, giving me a judging look. I couldn't decide if he was trying to signal I should have gone with jeans or if he was just in his typical not-a-morning-cat mood. He wasn't the only one who could be surly in the morning. "Try not to knock anything else over."

After I grabbed my bag off the hope chest at the foot of the four-poster bed, I jogged as quickly as I dared down the stairs and tried not to look in the direction of the living room, since I was certain no helpful elves had come to tidy up overnight.

I gripped the doorknob, reminding myself to be careful to watch where I was stepping on the porch. No need to repeat last night's almost-falling-through-the-floor experience.

Maybe things would look better this morning.

Once safely on the ground, I turned back to face the house, keeping my eyes tightly closed as if I were readying myself to be the guest of honor at a surprise party, desperately hoping it would somehow improve with the golden daylight shining against the windows. After all, things always seemed gloomy in the middle of the night— especially after driving for eleven hours. The cool, honeysuckle-scented breeze helped to both calm me down and give me just a hint of hope, so I opened my eyes.

What felt like a hundred pound weight dropped onto my shoulders, and my chin drooped in defeat. If anything, the old Victorian house looked worse now that it wasn't hidden beneath the cloak of darkness. Once-robin's egg blue paint peeled from the siding. Sections of the intricate woodwork were missing. Almost-black sections of plywood were hammered where stained glass windows had once gleamed.

How the hell had Kate let this happen? She was a historian for pity's sake. This was the Polk House.

49

The. Polk. House.

It should have been part of the town's scenic tour with a historical marker mounted on the front porch, not this wreck. I was surprised the ladies of the Preservation Society hadn't commanded my mom return to fix this not-so-little issue.

After all, this wasn't just the home place of the Polks. Its history as the town's stop along the Underground Railroad held significance for the entire South, if not the entire country. Knowing I was connected to something this valuable had always made my history-nerd heart go pitter patter. Now it made me sick.

And even without the Underground Railroad, the Polk House should have been carefully preserved. The town's charter was signed here by members of the three original families.

Then the realization hit me. Now all the Polks were gone. My eyes prickled with tears I didn't expect, and my throat felt scratchy as if I were catching a cold. No Polks. I knew I didn't count. What would happen now?

A rooster crowed in the distance, pulling me from my thoughts. I swiped at my nose with the sleeve of my hoodie, surprised at the unexpected wave of emotion. I didn't live here. I shouldn't care what happened to the town. I was just here to fix the mess Kate had left us with.

But first I still had to deal with the breakfast situation. I turned toward the gravel driveway while I zipped my hoodie against the cool morning, getting ready for a heck of a walk. I stopped in shock.

My truck was parked in the middle of the gravel driveway. I hadn't heard anyone coming or going. So how had it gotten here? It couldn't exactly drive itself.

I cautiously peeked through the passenger window. The keys hung from the ignition, definitely on the List of Things Not to Do in New Orleans, but I guess it was okay in Devil's Vale.

Thankful to realize I had a way to get into town that didn't involve my feet, I almost left right then. But I remembered Franklin and a certain dilemma—only my cat could be too housebroken. I placed a foot on my truck's battered bumper and hoisted myself high enough to reach the bed of the truck. I leaned over as far as I could reach, and my fingers still barely brushed against the plastic crate I needed—a drawback of being five-two. The rest of this stuff could wait: boxes of disposable gloves, cartons of tissue paper, extra waterproof bins. I stared at the box of masks my dad tossed in the back of the truck at the last second.

Either he was psychic or he must have suspected something like this. A word of warning would have been nice.

I grabbed Franklin's litter box out of the cab, hurried back inside the house to drop it off, and headed back out. Surely the little bakery would be open now. I could use a muffin or something for breakfast. If driving through the darkened streets last night had been any hint about the town's general activity level, Devil's Vale practically defined sleepy Southern town, and I hoped my guess was right. After my meeting with Tall, Dark and Muscular followed by my run-in with the chicken feeder, I wasn't really feeling up to too much small talk.

Driving down Main Street felt weirder in daylight. In the darkness, it had simply been one closed shop after another, and all were varying shades of brown and gray. With sunlight streaming down, it seemed like a town that time forgot. It could have been a Norman Rockwell painting.

Vintage cars lined the sides of the road. The mom-and-pop grocery store stood next to a diner that looked like it would have been happy in the movie *Grease*. I passed the post office just as one of the starched-uniform-wearing men headed out on his rounds...on foot. He didn't look anything like the lady with dreadlocks who delivered the mail back home.

God, what had I gotten myself into? Or should the question have been when? I held my phone up. Four bars. Cell reception still worked. Obviously, I didn't drive through a time portal with the fog. This town was weird.

There it was—Mugs, the town's bakery. The charming little house was almost directly in the center of Main Street painted a shocking shade of yellow that definitely wasn't on the list approved by any historical registry—so bright that even the most caffeine-deprived visitor would have little trouble finding it. My mom's description was spot-on, and it definitely seemed like the perfect little breakfast place. Apparently she wasn't the only one to think so, though. My stomach threatened to stage a revolt as I realized just how crowded it was.

I didn't really do crowds.

My hands started to sweat and slip off the steering wheel just thinking about making small talk. While my inner introvert tried to convince the rest of me that the granola bar in my bag would make a healthy, if less-than-satisfying breakfast, I dried my palms on my jeans and thought about cinnamon rolls, scones, and diner-strong coffee. I wouldn't get any of those by retreating into Kate's shop, even if I would find the peace and quiet I desperately wanted right now.

At least I hoped Daze Gone By would be peaceful. Judging by the condition of Kate's house, I might be a little too optimistic about her shop right now. My stomach gurgled, and I recognized the just-faintly-lightheaded feeling that accompanied mornings I tried to skip breakfast. Apparently, I'd spent too much time thinking about breakfast treats.

There was no turning back now. I was going to have to brave the bakery. I waited as a station wagon pulled out from the driveway in front of Mugs. The shop was so busy that cars were circling like vultures. Since parking seemed to be in limited supply, I turned into the lot across the street—the one that ran in front of my new, second home-away-from-home, taking just a second to look at Kate's store.

Gravel crunched under my truck's tires as it rocked to a stop. Kate must have just had the lot resurfaced. That was a good sign. Hopefully, the store wasn't in the same state of disrepair as the house. If Daze Gone By was in an equal state of disrepair as the house, I was grabbing Franklin and going home. Broken leg or not, my mom could do this job...later, after she was up and around again. If the bank needed the place cleared out before then, they could hire someone.

From the mums planted in front of the crawl space under the house to the ivory lace curtains visible through the darkened windows, Daze Gone By was the picture of a quaint antique store. She even had a row of white, wooden rocking chairs lining the covered porch for guests to sit and relax if they needed a break while walking from store to store. Those chairs wouldn't last a night back home, but with each passing minute, it became all the more clear that I definitely wasn't in New Orleans anymore.

One of the lace curtains inside the building stirred as if caught in a breeze, but when I squinted at the window, it seemed to be tightly shut. Maybe she'd left the air conditioner on inside, although I'd be surprised if it was running this morning. I'd been cold since I got to town. Not a physical cold, one that I could keep away with a jacket and a mug of hot chocolate. This chill was internal. Impenetrable. I'd had this feeling before.

I stared at the curtains. Now they were all perfectly still. Too still. If the air conditioner had blown them, at least one should still be moving. My nerves felt as raw as if someone had just dragged nails across a chalkboard, and my heart pounded, urging me to run—get out now while I still could.

The curtain didn't move. It was just a trick of the light on the glass. I was just starving. That was it. My blood sugar was low. I gave my head a good shake. I was letting hunger get to me.

I couldn't just sit here in my truck any longer. I was already drawing curious looks from the customers leaving the shop next door. Satisfied smiles turned to suspicion when they caught a glimpse of me in the truck. Not that I blamed them. I was new to town. I was sitting in a parked truck in front of the store where Aunt Kate had died. Locals probably thought I was casing the place.

Did they even have robberies in Devil's Vale?

Might as well get it over with and mingle with the locals. Maybe then they wouldn't be suspicious that something unnatural had happened to my aunt. Her death seemed normal. After all, she'd been almost a hundred.

But I knew how small towns worked. Somewhere someone was probably whispering that it seemed awfully suspicious. Kate had been in fine shape. Yep, so fine that her house was filled floor-to-ceiling with stuff.

But no real trash. Just stuff—boxes, crates, and piles of it.

That was weird.

Every other time I'd helped clean a house with a hoarder, the smell of rotting garbage, bug waste, and sometimes even the occasional dead animal combined to create an overwhelming and nauseating odor that even three showers couldn't fight. The smell would linger in my nose for days.

Aunt Kate's house smelled fine. A little musty, maybe, but nothing beyond the normal, old-house smell. The kitchen was clean. So was the bathroom. The sheets on the bed even smelled like fabric softener.

That had been unexpected.

I crossed the street on foot, pulled by the scent of baked goods. In a memory gone black-and-white, my mother had bought my birthday cake from Mugs back when I was in first or second grade. She must have been a repeat customer. We had enough mugs from Mugs for a dozen people to have coffee at our house, and they'd all have the matching souvenirs.

As I approached the front door, I heard the crowd before I saw them. The pleasant hum of excited conversation leaked out the windows and door, and I almost ran back to the store. But then I caught a whiff of coffee. I was hooked.

The door opened with a jingle, and the foyer was packed as I'd predicted from the number of cars outside. The line to order at the counter was long enough that it could have doubled for a line at an amusement park. Still, I'd come too far to turn back. Not when I could smell cinnamon, pecans, and maybe a hint of orange. One glance in the direction of the glass display case, and I met my downfall.

Chocolate-chocolate muffins.

Yep, line or not, I was staying. Aunt Kate's shop wasn't exactly going anywhere.

I took my place in the queue, trying not to count how many people were in front of me. Where had all these people come from anyway? I'd noticed the street was packed as I pulled in front of Kate's shop, but did everyone visiting town need to stop in at Mugs?

Then I noticed the clock on the wall. It was barely past 7:30. All the people here, with their maps and oversized bags tucked on their shoulders, distinctly smacked of tourists. If they were just here for the day, there wasn't much else to do but eat breakfast. Maybe a few of them should have just eaten at home.

My stomach rumbled, and I realized just how long it had been since I'd eaten anything. I made a mental note to find something resembling a grocery store before heading back to Kate's house tonight. I wasn't going to wait in this line again tomorrow if I could help it.

I had to give credit to the staff behind the counter. The line moved with the efficiency of the best restaurant back home. Honestly, the service seemed faster than what I was used to. As I closed in on my turn to order, I took a quick peek at the dining area.

Mugs was bigger than it looked. A lot bigger, really. What looked like a tiny, storefront bakery from the street had been turned into a full-sized restaurant through the years. The seating area was at least triple the size of the front bakery.

"And how can I help you?" A woman with curly hair who'd obviously had way too much caffeine this morning practically leaped to a stop in front of me.

I pointed to the tray of muffins on the bottom shelf. "One of those chocolate muffins and some coffee, please."

"Chocolate-chocolate. My favorite." She smiled indulgently, reaching for a sheet of waxed paper. She'd been doing this for a while. She had the talking-with-the-tourists voice down pat. "So, are you in town for Heritage Days too?"

That explained all the visitors. Three weeks spent reliving the town's less-than-always-genteel past. Kate talked about it every year. Civil War buffs arrived from around the country to watch the battle reenactments, visit the historic homes, and take the candlelight tour of the stops along the Underground Railroad. The almost month-long experience culminated in some kind of town-wide party. Kate never missed it. She was even a tour guide for the candlelight tour. Of course, I'd have to arrive in town during the whole Heritage Days mess. I couldn't think of anything I'd like to do less.

56

I tried not to show my distaste for the festival when I answered the woman with a firmer-than-it-should-be, "No."

She squinted and blinked at me. I was an oddity, someone she didn't recognize, someone not in town for the same reason everyone else was. "I don't think I've seen you before."

"Probably not."

"Then what brings you to town?"

I might as well be honest. Since Kate's shop was across the street, we'd be seeing each other often. Daily, if she was the stare-out-the-lace-windows type. And, judging by her questions, she was. I might as well head off gossip before it got too out of control. "I'm here to settle my aunt's estate."

Her eyes widened in shock. "You're Kate's kin?"

"Yep." I forced a smile I didn't feel. I should have just gone with the granola bar so I wouldn't have had to play Twenty Questions. Behind me, the customers were beginning to grumble about the sudden slowdown in service.

"So sorry to hear about her passing. Your aunt was a lovely lady. Really contributed to the town." She seemed genuinely sad. She poured a cup of coffee, adding it to the tray with my plated muffin, and then bypassed the cash register. "On the house."

"I can pay."

"I know you can. Just being neighborly. My name's Mabel."

"I'm Reese." I fumbled an attempt at an introductory handshake when she wrapped me in a too-tight hug. "And thanks."

"No need." She swatted away the thanks like she was batting away a fly. "I own this place. You just let me know if I

57

can help you with anything. We're all family 'round here. You just holler if you need some help. I can rustle up some high school boys if you need help movin' anything heavy." She pressed the tray into my hands with a firmness that suggested I shouldn't argue about the whole free thing.

"I'll remember that." I took the tray, but she'd already begun to focus on her next customer. So Mabel owned Mugs. I hoped I wouldn't need to ask for help, but since I wasn't sure of the condition of Kate's place, it wouldn't hurt to have a friend in town.

I took my tray to the dining area. In places like these, locals tended to be territorial about their seats. And visitors traveled in packs. My seating options were limited to an empty booth that would probably seat six, and likely earn me glares from the wait staff, and an oversized table looking out the window that screamed 'I'm eating alone.'

But the problem was there was only one seat open at the window seating, and it was directly next to one of two people in town who I'd already met. Tall, Dark, and Muscular was going to think I was stalking him.

"Good morning." I took the spot, biting the bullet and making contact with him, wincing as my words came out far cheerier than I'd hoped.

"It's you." Not exactly a greeting. His face showed he was caught as off guard as I was. With papers spread partially onto my section of the long table, he clearly wasn't expecting company this morning, least of all me.

"I didn't get a chance to thank you."

"No problem. I was heading into town last night anyway and couldn't leave you stranded."

"Oh." I gave him what I hoped was a friendly smile. "That too, but I was talking about bringing my truck back this morning. You didn't have to do it."

58

"It wasn't any trouble." He'd started shuffling the pages into a stack. Without intending to pry, I saw a boarding pass for a flight leaving later this morning. Funny. He didn't look like a Maxwell Graves. No wonder he'd said to just call him Max. Maxwell seemed too sophisticated for a guy who looked like he could jump you in a back alley.

Graves. Then it hit me. He was a Graves? I hadn't seen that one coming.

And now I was staring. First I was the Damsel in Distress. Now I'd moved on to Creepy, Staring, Stalker Chick. *Smooth, Everett, very smooth.*

"But still." I pointed to the plane ticket in his pile. "You have better things to do."

"It's not a problem." He answered like he was annoyed with me for thanking him. "I've got to be going."

"Have a good flight."

An almost-pained grimace washed over his face. "Thanks."

"Oh, and by the way, what was wrong with my truck?"

"What?" He stuffed his papers into a bag I hadn't noticed at his feet. It looked like he was already packed and ready to fly out.

"My truck. Why wouldn't it start? I'd just had it tuned-up before I left. I want to yell at the guys at the shop for missing something."

"Your battery cable came loose. It was an easy fix. Don't blame them." He lied with a surprising smoothness. "Goodbye."

He turned and walked away, leaving me with questions I hadn't had just last night. The battery cable wasn't loose.

I'd tested them when the truck stopped. So why did he lie about what was wrong with my truck?

I ate my meal in silence. No one else came to sit next to me. Either no other singles arrived at the bakery or I was wearing a Do Not Approach Me sign. It didn't matter. I wasn't in the mood for more conversation, and the more I delayed going to the shop, the more my stomach grumbled with nerves.

After popping the last bite in my mouth, I picked up my bag, headed out the side door, and jogged across the street to the blue-framed old house. The banister was painted a deep powder blue, contrasting nicely with the sky blue of the rest of the building. Kate definitely must have had a thing for blue. I tried not to notice that the trim was almost the exact color of the chicken guy's eyes last night.

I blinked. Where had that thought come from? But, yes, the more I studied the paint color, the more I was sure it would be a pretty close match. Was that kind of blue in someone's eyes even real?

His eyes weren't the only thing about him that didn't seem real. I'd gotten a pretty decent look at him while he was passed out on Kate's couch. His jacket had sagged open, revealing a white t-shirt stretched so tight it practically screamed that he worked out. While his jeans were dirty like he'd been doing some kind of manual labor, they were designer—the kind cut to show muscle underneath the fabric. And they definitely did their job.

Nope. Not going there. I was not in the market at all. Definitely not shopping around here. Besides, what was I doing? I hid my face behind my hands. Was I really stooping so low to be ogling him when he'd been unconscious? I was going to hell for this.

I glanced around for something to distract me, swallowing down an overwhelming rush of embarrassment as I felt a rush of color flooding my cheeks. I didn't deserve to think about him. No, the neighbor guy was off limits.

After all, I'd probably given him a concussion. What had I been thinking? This wasn't some sketchy downtown. No random creep would have been skulking in the middle of my chicken coop.

There was no time to stand here thinking about the guy I'd managed to literally knock out. I needed to get inside and get to work. I was lucky he hadn't called the police. I mean, I was justified since he was on my property—well, Kate's property—but he apparently was supposed to be there.

I hoped I'd never see him again. I took a quick peek over my shoulder, not sure what I was expecting. In a town this size, that wasn't going to happen, but that didn't mean he was lurking around the shop.

Pull yourself together, Everett. So far, nothing about this trip had gone as planned. But today was a fresh start. All I had to do was go inside, survey what inventory Kate had on hand, and report back to my parents.

Simple. Easy.

Right.

I crossed the porch. Not a single plank squeaked, another good sign. I paused in front of the door.

The only problem with carrying a big purse was it was big. My keys liked to play a game with me. They'd hide, and I had to seek. I groaned. I'd just had them in my hands. Just before I was going to have to resort to emptying my bag, my fingers connected with the metal ring.

Finally. I placed my key in the lock, and it turned without a hitch.

I turned the knob, opening the door a crack. The all-too-familiar scent of mothballs, mold, and the almost-vanilla fragrance of aging paper rushed out to greet me.

"You're going to keep it open, right?" a thick-as-honey drawl called up from the bottom step behind me. I'd been so lost in my thoughts I hadn't even heard my visitor walking up the gravel path. She didn't look older than me. Why was she out so early in the morning?

"We haven't decided yet." I tried to keep my voice as light and friendly as hers.

"This place has been here for years. I don't know what Main Street would be like without it."

Her face was mostly hidden beneath a veil of corn silk-yellow hair as she gave me a demure smile that seemed like it had been practiced in front of the mirror. Her eyelashes fluttered Southern-debutante style, and her crystal-blue-eyed stare almost took my breath away.

Unsettled, I rubbed the back of my neck, fighting for composure for the second time of the morning. I didn't understand why a knot settled in the pit of my stomach.

"Surely you need to carry on the family business."

I fought back a laugh. If the residents of Devil's Vale knew what our family business was, they'd probably drive me out of here with pitchforks and torches. No, I wasn't carrying on the family business.

"Oh, I'm sorry. I'm being rude." She spoke with a charm that seemed oddly genuine or well-practiced. Either she was honestly sorry or she should have gone into acting. She extended her hand in my direction as a peace offering. "My name's Shelby. Shelby Waters. You're Reese, right?"

"Right." I shook her hand, surprised at the chill that ran up my arm, leaving a trail of goosebumps in its wake. A shudder clawed its way up my spine.

The Waters. The Polks. The Graves.

Each family line was still represented in Devil's Vale today. I remembered hearing Kate talking about town comings and goings with my mother on speakerphone during one of the all-too-frequent conversations asking when Mom was coming back. They typically met with a comment hinting that we'd return sometime beyond never.

This too-perky-to-live neighbor was a Waters?

Kate's tone of voice when she'd said the last name never really inspired an overly close relationship with any of them, and now one just magically popped up who knew my name.

"I get it. You're stuck on the whole Waters thing, right?"

She could read my mind too. Charming.

Shelby dropped her head, but not before I saw her eyebrows raise and a grin beginning to stretch across her cheeks. After a moment's pause from the joke I hadn't heard, she looked back up at me while plucking at her collar as if it had just become too hot. "So I take it Kate didn't really spared any details."

No, Kate had spared a great many details.

"We're not all as bad as the rumors make us out to be." Her eyes rolled up toward the haint-blue ceiling on the porch like she was considering something. "Well, maybe my dad. We just try to ignore him."

I couldn't tell if she was teasing or not.

Shelby didn't let my hesitation or nonresponse slow me down. "I just feel like I know you already. Kate was always talking about you." She paused and took a breath that didn't

63

feel like it was acting. "And she had your picture in her office. I own the candle shop next door."

"You're the other night owl in town!" My voice sounded a tad too enthusiastic.

"Night owl?"

"Last night when I came through town, I saw your light on."

"Oh." She smiled like she knew a secret but didn't plan to share. "Yes, I do have a tendency to work late. It's easier to concentrate without customers."

"I'm sure it is."

The glint in her eyes sent a prickle up my spine. Stop being so melodramatic. This might be your only friend in town.

Before I could think of anything else to say, Shelby started backing across the parking lot. "Well, I won't keep you. Just wanted to drop in and say hello. I know you must have a lot to do."

A lot to do? That was an understatement. "Nice to meet you."

"You too." She nodded and waved. "I'm sure we'll be seeing each other again soon."

Time seemed to slow as she made her way between the two buildings, and a chill filled the air around me. I couldn't shake the sense that Shelby was more than she appeared.

That made two of us.

I stood on the porch for longer than I should have. Part of me wanted to run, while part of me was frozen, overwhelmed with a sudden sense of responsibility. Shelby's comments haunted me. Daze Gone By meant something to the life of the town. I could almost feel the life force pulsing through the floorboards beneath my feet.

The muscles in my shoulders tensed, and an unexpected sense of foreboding buzzed around me like a gnat. I couldn't see it, and I couldn't make it go away. I tossed my head like a horse shaking off a fly.

I went back to what I was doing before Shelby's interruption. How had she met me on the porch anyway? Was she a card-carrying member of the nosy-neighbor society? Did she have a camera trained on the parking lot?

Unless I wanted to run after her and ask, which I didn't, standing around asking myself pointless questions wasn't going to get me anywhere. I tried to shake off the things-aren't-quite-right feelings, but they were as difficult to shed as a spider web.

At least for now, I was going to need to ignore the Waters issue. Shelby was a neighbor, a friend of Kate's. She was doing what people in these little towns do. And right now I had more than enough to do.

Compared to the house, the shop was in pristine condition. Other than a little dust, it could have been any antique store or consignment shop I'd visited through the years. That probably warranted a text to my mother. I hadn't called yet this morning, and since she had the uncanny ability to call right when I was on the top of a ladder, I might as well check in to avoid an ill-timed phone call.

I pulled my phone out of my pocket and swiped to wake it up. At the shop. Things look pretty good. Better than the house. I'll be working on inventory. Forgot to charge my phone. It'll be plugged in. I'll call tonight.

I hadn't forgotten to charge my phone, and it wasn't going to be plugged in. But she didn't need to know that. I dug a composition book out of my bag to use taking inventory.

The hot, muggy air hung thick around me. The stench of stillness signaled the air conditioner likely hadn't run during the whole time past Kate's death—not a good sign. If the heat had been this oppressive for more than a few days, I was guaranteed to discover more than a few of the shop's more delicate items were trash bin fodder.

I was so caught up in ruminating about the heat, I almost missed it. Out of the corner of my eye, I caught the faintest sway from the ivory curtains. While the motion wouldn't be described in a little-old-lady-staring-at-the-neighbors way, it also couldn't be simply dismissed in the room that was definitely breeze deficient.

A thin band of sweat formed along my lip that had nothing to do with the heat. If the air conditioner hadn't been running, what had made the curtains move? I let my eyes slowly roam the room, using both common sight and the sight that would allow me a peek into things generally left unseen.

Nothing.

Nothing other than a blasting headache. And not just a small one. One that threatened to make me see nonexistent fireworks any second. My stomach roiled, and I dropped to a seat in a chair that didn't look authentic, closing my eyes.

The headache receded as quickly as an evening tide. Gradually, my stomach stopped feeling like I was a passenger on a ship in the midst of a hurricane. I gingerly picked my hand up from the armrest of the chair, hoping my snap assessment of the chair's value had been correct.

I squinted at the stitching. Too regular to be hand-sewn. And the styling of the chair suggested it was made in the Civil War era. Definite reproduction. A sigh of relief flowed through me as I once again took in my surroundings, choosing to ignore the fluttering curtains for the moment. I'd probably just imagined them, a side effect of low blood sugar or something like that.

The front of the shop was decorated like an old music room, complete with antique player piano. I hadn't seen one of those in ages. I walked up to it, running my hand over the almost-mahogany finish of the wood, and I remembered Kate had one almost identical to it at her house. I wondered if either still worked. I'd have to check tonight.

ॐ

I was beyond tired when I pulled into the gravel driveway back at Kate's house. I hadn't quite worked until sundown, but I'd come close. Exhaustion mixed with loneliness clouded my vision as I put the truck in park, and I almost didn't see chicken guy sitting on Kate's porch.

But when I noticed him, I almost put the truck into reverse to leave, no idea where I was headed. I just didn't want to deal with him tonight. I'd already apologized once. Still, it didn't feel like quite enough after knocking someone out for what felt like hours.

I was trapped in the midst of indecision when the guy stood and beckoned me toward Kate's porch. That's when I noticed the two paper bags sitting next to him. He'd brought food.

My stomach rumbled and won the battle, against my better judgment.

He grinned broadly and gave a fake half duck when I opened the door. "No bats?"

"It wasn't a bat last time." I answered with more suspicion than the situation probably needed. By this time, the scent of french fries carried on the breeze. "Why are you here?"

"Thought you might be hungry." He tilted his head to the side, displaying a grin so charming it should be illegal. One shoulder drew up in a dismissive shrug, and he

67

squinted with a flirty wink that likely got his dates to agree to anything he asked. "And Kate paid me to be here."

That stopped me in my tracks. "She paid you? For what?"

"She thought my services might be of use around here."

"Your services?" I couldn't help it if my mind flickered to unclean thoughts. I didn't need glasses to be able to tell the guy was exactly my type—dirty blond hair, eyes too blue for description. A body built well enough to be an actor on *Friday Night Lights*. Since he'd been mumbling about being tackled without a helmet, I figured he even played the game. I could think of a few services he could offer.

He cleared his throat, reminding me he was still standing next to me, and I felt a rush of redness flood my face.

"Can we go in? I'd rather not eat the burgers on the porch."

"Burgers?"

"Do you repeat everything someone says to you, or do you just not speak Southern?"

"I guess I'm just trying to figure out why it sounded like you had two." This guy was probably a player at his school. I'd seen his keychain with an unfamiliar fraternity emblem hanging out of his pocket last night.

"I thought you might be hungry. You've been gone all day."

"How do you know I've been gone?"

"I spent most of it on your porch, which, by the way is definitely hot enough to keep the fries hot, so I wouldn't say no to some air conditioning."

He tossed the hint with the subtlety I'd expect from someone who thought it was perfectly normal to feed someone else's chickens after ten o'clock at night. This presented a problem. I knew his kind. That's why I absolutely didn't want anything else to do with him, but I couldn't exactly walk around him and leave him outside—especially since he'd brought dinner. I could, but not without making Kate rise up from the grave to slap me over the head for being less than neighborly.

I summoned my best attempt at hospitality. "Would you like to come inside?"

"I thought you'd never ask." He followed me through the door but then led the way to the table in the kitchen like he'd been in the house before. I guess that shouldn't have surprised me. Anyone who'd drive up in the middle of the night to feed the chickens probably knew Kate. "I'm guessing she didn't tell you about me."

Did Kate tell me she had a looking-at-him-would-melt-your-chocolate hot neighbor? No. I took the bag of french fries he offered, placing them on top of a folded napkin, and tried to decide if I needed to stick my head in the refrigerator to cool off. "Tell me about you?"

"You're doing that thing again." He bit his lip in an attempt not to laugh at me, but his lips still tilted up in a smirk, revealing a hint of a dimple in his cheek.

Why couldn't I think straight in his presence? It was like I was the one of us who had the probable concussion. I cleared my throat, trying not to sound too eager. "Kate asked you to do something?" And then it hit me. "You're the neighbor. The one the lawyer said would be helping out around the house. They'd hired you or something."

He looked honestly amused. "A lawyer? No. That'd be your aunt."

"But Mrs. Smith said she contacted you."

69

"Mrs. Smith gave me the key. That's all." He reached into the bag and pulled out his waxed-paper wrapped hamburger. "But Kate called me while I was back in Augusta. She said she knew I'd be out on summer break and she had a list of things for me to do. She didn't really give me much say in the whole thing." He took an oversized bite of burger, and a dab of ketchup clung to his lower lip. "Typical Kate."

I didn't need to be staring at his lips. I was only here for one reason—to clean up Kate's stuff. I didn't need any other mess, especially not one of the male variety.

He chewed and swallowed loudly. Definite jock.

"She called me one night out of the blue and told me the house needed a few repairs." He looked around the room, and I couldn't tell if he was rolling his eyes or just studying the place. "She read me a list over the phone and said I needed to start today."

"Today?" I winced at the repetition and coughed into my fist. "She was that specific?"

"You're still doing that weird repeat thing." He covered his mouth with his hand as he explained through a mouthful of fries. "Do I need to use smaller words?"

"No." My annoyance meter clicked up a notch. This guy might be cute, but he didn't get to make fun of me.

"I'm detecting some hesitation. If you don't want me here, I can sign the check over to Bud from town, but I think he's using a walker now. It would be kind of cruel to make him work on his hands and knees."

Dude who was cute and knew it or a guy who was a member of AARP. Kind of a tough call.

"I figure you're going to want to sell the place. Can't have people touring the house falling through the porch.

That wouldn't be a way to welcome them. So what do you say?"

I took a drink of my soda. Cute and cocky dude it was. Of course, there was still the small matter that I didn't know who he was.

"So, me or Bud?"

"First, one more thing." A hint of suspicion colored his eyes. "If you're going to be my new handyman, do I get to find out your name?"

"Sorry." Now it was his turn to blush. "Guess I forgot to introduce myself. That sometimes happens when I get knocked out." He held out a hand in proper Southern greeting. "My name's Colton. And you are?"

"I'm Reese. Reese Everett."

"Not a Polk?"

"Kate was my great-aunt on my mother's side, so I guess it depends how specific you want to get."

"I'm fine with Everett." He inclined his head in an almost-bow. "Nice to meet you, Reese Everett."

"Well, Colton, technically, Kate hired you, but now it's official. Good luck with this place. I think you're going to need it."

As if to reinforce the point, a bang shot through the house. Franklin went from dead asleep at my feet to fur-on-end, standing on top of the refrigerator before I had time to swallow. One bang would have been fine, easy to dismiss. Something had just fallen upstairs.

The footsteps were harder to explain.

"Did you hear that?" Colton was on his feet, eyes peering at the ceiling.

"Something fell." No longer hungry, I placed the hamburger back on the paper towel. "With all the stuff Kate has piled up, we're lucky the ceiling hasn't caved in."

Colton was breathing fast now, and his face had paled to a pasty shade of white. His muscles were tensed, and he seemed to be one footstep away from sprinting out of the kitchen.

I recognized his behavior. Our tour guests acted the same way when we made the mistake of treading into too up-close-and-personal territory of the supernatural kind. I hadn't figured Colton would be a believer. Judging from the way he was sweating and his eyes darted around the room, he didn't know he was a believer either.

"Is someone upstairs?" He wasn't buying the something-just-fell story.

Until I had a better sense of exactly what else was in the house, I wasn't going exploring with him. I'd met plenty of spirits in my day. Some could be reasoned with. Others...well, those were best handled when I was alone.

"There's no one upstairs, unless someone slipped in while you were getting burgers. You think someone might have broken in to get their hands on one of Kate's treasures?" I thumbed toward the living room and forced my voice to stay light, to sound like I was teasing. The footsteps were louder now. Definitely more pronounced. They seemed to be centered directly above our heads. "I wish whoever it is luck."

"You seriously don't hear that?" Now Colton's arms were rigid at his side, his hands white-knuckled and fisted.

"No." I lied. I was a great liar. I'd had lots of practice. "I'm kind of tired. I think I'm going to call it an early night."

I prayed he'd take the hint. He didn't.

Now he was walking through the room, keeping his eyes on the beadboard ceiling and taking care to stay directly below the footsteps. Whoever was upstairs was pacing. I could tell since he appeared to be copying the movements right in front of me.

"There's someone moving up there. I can't just leave you here."

Awesome. The one time I wanted to get rid of a guy, he has to pull a you-need-a-strong-guy-to-protect-you act.

I shrugged, trying to appear nonchalant. No one had mentioned that Kate's house was haunted. And I definitely didn't remember running into any *friends* back when I used to live here. "Should we go upstairs?"

He definitely didn't seem like he wanted to, but he was also unwilling to have me show him up.

"Stay behind me." Colton waved me back from my position at his side, and I had to work hard to stay in the role of innocent Southern belle when I wanted to shove him out of my way and climb the stairs two at a time before I missed my chance to see who I was sharing the house with. "Can I have that thing you hit me with?"

I fought back a laugh as I hurried to the fireplace. I took hold of the iron shovel, knowing full well that this wasn't going to help him, not unless he was just trying to tickle the ghost, but I carried it to him anyway. Whatever made him feel better.

We snaked through the dining room, living room, and up the stairs, me close on his heels. Once we left the kitchen, the footsteps either went away or were simply too soft to hear. I hoped for the latter since I wanted to catch a glimpse of my houseguest. I'd save the conversation for later—when we didn't have company.

73

The hallway was dark and felt too narrow. I should have left a light on this morning, but I hadn't thought it would get this dark this fast. He led the way past Kate's bedroom. I tried not to cringe at the mess I'd left. The next two rooms were so filled with boxes, no one was getting inside until after I'd cleared them out. That only left one room.

Colton hesitated in front of the closed door. It had been open when I left this morning, of that I was certain. I remembered seeing the sunlight streaming amid the boxes in what looked like it once was a library or some type of study. The muscles in his jaw tensed as he reached for the doorknob.

He was beyond freaked out, but he wasn't going to admit it.

"Doorknob stuck?" I pushed past him, hoping I could put both of us out of our misery. "Let me try."

The glass knob turned with ease, and the door opened of its own accord, revealing the same hodgepodge smattering of boxes I'd noticed this morning.

I hadn't remembered leaving a lamp on, and the window hadn't appeared to be lit when I pulled into the driveway earlier tonight. Maybe I just hadn't noticed. I stepped into the room, turning in a tight circle as I studied my surroundings—deep blue wallpaper, wall-to-wall shelves so packed they bowed under the weight of leather-bound books, family portraits of people I didn't have the slightest clue who they were.

No ghost.

"It's empty." Colton sounded honestly surprised.

"Is sneaking into other people's houses common around here?" I hid my disappointment inside the question.

"Not exactly."

"That's promising to hear." I shoved my hands into the pockets of my jeans. "But I really am tired. Unless you're planning on joining me..."

A flush rushed to my cheeks, and I hoped he was too distracted to notice. What the hell was happening to me? I hadn't had a date since my junior year, and that ended so badly I'd considered joining a convent. We weren't even Catholic.

"Um. No." Colton pursed his lips like the suggestion was the worst one he'd heard in years. Way to make a girl feel good about herself. At least I didn't have to worry about him trying to hit on me while he was working. "I'll see you tomorrow."

Now things felt even more still and awkward. I should probably get an award for least likely to ever date again.

"Yeah." I nodded, trying to redeem the night. "And thanks for the burgers."

"Any time." His eyes were a little too wide as he gave the room one last cursory glance before he stepped around me, leaving me alone in the upstairs hallway.

I let myself lean back, thudding against the doorframe. I might not understand why I hadn't seen my guest yet, but I knew I was far from alone.

જ્જ

Classical music echoed off the walls of the room. Caught in the half sleep from staying awake far beyond midnight, I tumbled out of bed and onto the floor. Kate had a working alarm clock hidden around here somewhere?

Typical.

Crap. Too dark to see the details of the room, I felt around for any hint at how to turn the music off.

Even Franklin was ticked off. He hissed, and I knew that if I could see him, he'd be standing on the foot of the bed with his back arched so high he was risking hurting himself. He spat into the air.

This was one ticked-off cat.

Not that I could really blame him. It had taken hours to go to sleep tonight. An alarm sounding before dawn was the last thing I needed.

The music swelled in intensity. I recognized a string of notes Kate half-hummed, half-sang the last time she came to visit Mom. This station must play that song a lot. Finally, my eyes had started to adjust to the lack of light—hairbrush, book, pile of pens, notepad.

I turned to look at the other nightstand. No radio. Empty, except for a tea cup that was probably ready to grow mold samples. I moved cleaning the bedroom up a few notches on my to-do list.

The music was loud. Too loud. I could feel the rumble of the low notes vibrating the mattress. Hearing was one of the first senses to go, but this was ridiculous. Kate must have been horrible at waking up with an alarm. She was like my roommate in college who had to put the alarm clock across the room in order to really wake up. Where had Kate hidden the clock?

I squinted into the darkness—piles of blankets, dirty clothes, a mostly empty desk. No clock.

Franklin's hissing had turned into an impression of a machine gun. He only reacted like that when...

No.

Hell no. The hair on the back of my neck arched up. There was a piano in the room off the foyer, wasn't there? I listened intently. This music was live—it didn't have the wispy edge that came from being played over the radio.

Crap.

Not one of *those* ghosts.

Random footsteps parading around upstairs was one thing. A ghost that kept me from sleeping at night was something totally different. This ghost and I were going to have to have a little chat. I slid my phone off the nightstand to glance at the time. Three a.m. Awesome. This ghost even decided to have the concert at the Devil's Hour. How appropriate.

I took hold of the doorknob, trying to ignore how unnaturally cold it was. Typically, ghosts didn't bother me, but I generally dealt with them after a decent night's sleep.

"You coming?" I arched an eyebrow in Franklin's direction. Suddenly, he was extremely comfortable on the bed. "Coward."

Wishing I'd thought to grab my flashlight, I carefully felt my way down the hallway. The music swelled in intensity.

My piano player had changed songs. I recognized a Bach piece an old boyfriend liked to pound out on Mom's perpetually out-of-tune piano.

"Hello?"

Never, ever surprise a ghost.

I hoped it was a just ghost. Some of the Polk family members had favored the darker arts.

"You're an excellent piano player." I wasn't lying. The tune changed again. For someone undead, this ghost had quite a repertoire. While I might not recognize this song, it was beautiful. Haunting, really. I chuckled to myself. A ghost playing a haunting melody. Sounded like a punch line in an old horror movie.

Now I was cracking myself up. I needed more sleep.

A sharp pain caught me just below the knee, and I fought the desire to cry out. Screaming wasn't going to do anything other than freak out my visitor. And a freaked-out ghost wasn't generally friendly.

"What song is that?" I didn't expect a reply, but stranger things had happened. Being more careful this time, I reached out in front of myself, sweeping my hands from side to side—a box on the right, another on the left.

A hint of a headache nudged at my temples. Something felt off. The more I tried to connect, the more everything seemed a little fuzzy.

After what felt like an hour but was probably just five minutes or so, I made it to the doorway to the music room. The song was loud now, the deep bass vibrating beneath my feet.

"I like your music." I rounded the corner, mentally preparing myself for what I was about to see.

But the room was dark and empty. I squinted, focusing intently. This just didn't happen. First the curtains at the antiques shop and now this. Two ghosts couldn't both hide from me...neither could one for that matter. I'd never had a ghost able to hide from me, not when I was really looking. Just seconds ago, the rhythm pounded beneath my feet. Supernatural or not, my piano-playing friend hadn't had time to escape.

A sharp, stabbing pain threatened to knock me to my knees. A soft breeze passed over my cheek. The ghost wasn't gone. I just couldn't see it.

That. Didn't. Happen.

"Where are you?" I squinted through the aura clouding my vision. "I know you're here. You don't have to be afraid. I just want to talk." A low ringing muffled my hearing. No matter how badly I wanted to focus, I couldn't.

The floor seemed to shift beneath my feet, and I had no choice but to kneel before I fell. I struggled to gain some degree of control, but the darkness continued to press in from every side. The more I fought, the more the velvety-blackness closed around me.

And then I saw nothing.

Time passed, and the near-deafening ringing in my ears faded away, leaving a sound reminiscent of listening to a sea shell. My eyes stung and felt as if I needed sunglasses even in the pre-morning grayness. The throbbing in my head dulled to a mild ache.

More than that, any sense I'd had of someone being in the room with me was gone. The stillness surrounding me was only interrupted by the soft thudding of Franklin's tail against the hardwood floor. Now he decided to come join me.

An odd scent lingered—cedar wood or pine. Something outdoorsy. Something that wasn't the musty, dusty scent of the living room and foyer.

Franklin had been right. We weren't alone in the house.

Chapter Six

Colton

I hesitated in the main house's front hallway. After being gone for so long, it still felt foreign for me to be back here now. It was odd to realize what once was so familiar was exactly what made me feel out of sync. The aroma of fried bacon, country-style potatoes, and almost too-sweet cinnamon rolls merged into the scent of the traditional Waters family Sunday morning breakfast. I glared at the french doors to the dining room standing open and waiting for me.

When I was away at school, I'd been free from the weekly summons. Only now did I realize just how good I'd had it. I could sleep until noon if I'd wanted, but even more than that, I didn't have to sit and stir my coffee under my father's scornful watch. So far, I'd managed to avoid the mandatory family breakfasts. I'd just gotten back in town and needed to unpack, then Max needed me, but I'd run out of excuses. Judging by the note my mother left tucked in the door of the cabin, avoiding the weekly gathering this morning would be a mistake.

So here I was. Trapped in the foyer. There was nothing like a trip to a home that could easily house a couple dozen people to make someone feel insignificant. The tinkling sound of silver striking against china signaled I was late— and no one was waiting for me.

Not even the idea of freshly baked cinnamon rolls could tempt me this morning.

"Will you be gracing us with your presence this morning?" My father's radar was on-point. Based on the English-bulldog glower on his face, he was already in rare form this morning. Breakfast was going to be fun.

"I'm here, aren't I?" I held my hands up in mock salute and was immediately annoyed with myself. I might be back in town now, living almost under his roof, but I was far beyond the little boy who let himself get kicked around by his father. And it was time for me to prove it.

My eyes met his in challenge, but he didn't say another word. Instead, he quickly looked away, flicking a glance back into the dining room. Mom must be waiting.

I made my way down the last section of the hall before turning into the dining room. The scent of coffee hung heavy in the air, making me wish I'd skipped the weekly summons and just driven to Mugs. At least there, I knew I'd be greeted by people who pretended to be happy to see me.

Stepping through the doorway was like stepping back in time. Somehow I doubted the almost-apricot painted walls had changed since my great-grandparents owned the house. I knew the floral tapestries hadn't changed. When I'd made the unfortunate mistake of playing hide and seek with Max, I'd received the first real punishment of my life for accidentally causing the tiniest hole possible in the fabric when my belt caught on the lining. Someone had to have examined the curtains with a magnifying glass to even find it. I still blamed my sister for that one. One of the maids caught her doing something off-limits in her bedroom, and pointing out my even graver error had proven to be too easy an escape to pass up.

The same pastels hung on either side of the gilded mirror, the canvas only slightly more tinted by age than when I was a toddler. The oversized floral arrangement looked like something straight out of one of my mother's interior design magazines. The mixture of hydrangeas, lavender, and sheep's ear was likely planted in the cutting garden just to accent the pictures on the dining room wall.

An oversized coffee urn sat on the console just like every other Sunday morning. At one point, the family was probably big enough to at least make a dent in the amount brewed for breakfast, but now it was just the four of us. I glanced around the room. Three of us. "Where's Shelby?"

"Some members of this family still know the definition of punctuality." My father pulled out his chair at the head of the table and took a seat. The already half-eaten pieces of bacon and square of cinnamon roll was a show they weren't content to wait for me.

"You mean she got in here early and then escaped."

"Watch your tongue." My mother's sterling silver spoon tinged against the china coffee cup. Breakfast now felt more like an ambush. Mom trained her too-sharp-to-be-sick eyes on me and trapped my gaze. I couldn't look away even if I wanted to. Now I understood why my friends hated being in her class at school. "When are you planning on telling us?"

From her tone of voice, she wasn't expecting a positive announcement. I hesitated, choosing to pick up a plate and take my time pondering my selections. I might not feel like eating breakfast, but neither of them had to know it. "Tell you what?"

"Come on. Don't take me for a fool. It's practically written all over your face." She sat up even straighter in her chair, looking like a bird of prey ready to launch at road kill beneath it. "Something happen back at school?"

"What makes you think that?"

"Colton." She used my name as a warning. "We should have gotten the bill from school by now."

"I had a full ride at school. Y'all weren't paying anything."

"I'm quite aware of your athletic scholarship. I was discussing medical school. Aren't you supposed to be starting in August? They should have sent us the bill for the first payment by now."

Caught because she paid the bills. Damn, could the day get off to a worse start? "I'm not going to medical school."

"What happened?" She spoke in the same soothing voice she once used when she told me they were putting my dog to sleep the next morning. I'd loved Duke. Just like I loved medicine. Or at least I thought I did.

"I don't know. One day, I'd been welcomed by the head of the school. A week later, I got a letter saying they regretted to inform me that I hadn't been selected. They'd sent out the acceptance letter by mistake."

"Why'd you wait to tell us?" Her fingers trembled as she traced the outline of her pearl necklace.

"Not exactly high on my list, I guess." I felt like a kindergartener who brought a note home from his teacher. "Y'all had already announced it in the paper. What was I supposed to do?"

"That was your mother's decision." Dad's voice boomed from his seat at the table. He'd seemed to be entranced by his phone, oblivious to the conversation going on around him, but now I realized he'd caught more than enough. He scowled as he cut a wedge from his cinnamon roll.

"The whole idea of medical school was a mistake. I always said you weren't cut out for something like that. Now just look. You're embarrassing the family." Dad stabbed the bite with deliberate slowness.

He was taunting me. Waiting for me to ask what my punishment would be, just like in middle school when my teacher had caught me peeking at another student's paper. I'd learned that night that I never wanted to get on his shit list again. I couldn't sit down for a week.

But here I was. Now I was bigger than him. I outweighed him too. He wouldn't be able to manage his old favorite punishments, but he could still make my life hell. Maybe I'd talk to Bud and send him out to work on Kate's house anyway. Then I could just leave.

"You don't have to worry about me shaming the family. I'll get packed up and be out by tonight. I can go back to my apartment and find a job back in Augusta."

"You'll do nothing of the sort. This is your home. You belong here." My mom shot my dad a look that told him he'd better back her up.

"You can't leave." He practically growled at me. "You've got a job to do. Didn't Kate already pay you?"

He waved his fork in the direction of the window. If I tilted my head just right, I could see the outline of Kate's roof through the trees. I should have taken a better look at it before I agreed to help. From the way it looked, I'd be lucky to be done by Christmas.

Dad wanted me to finish at Kate's? That was a shock. I'd barely mentioned the job to him. I figured being the hired help was beneath a Waters.

"You can stay out in the groundskeeper's cabin for the summer like we'd planned. Once you've finished this job, we'll find you something else." Just like always, Mom was already five steps ahead of me—trying to fix my problems, even if her solution wasn't what I wanted.

As long as her solution was what was best for the family, that's all that mattered. I hated being a Waters.

84

"I can talk with Rick too. He owes me a favor." Dad nodded, acting like the decision had already been made, but I wasn't sure if he was reassuring me or my mom. "They'll be needing a new football coach."

"Can you get any more crass? Seriously!"

"I'm just being practical."

Of course you are. Practically running my life as usual. The grass hadn't even grown over the grave yet. "Dad, I'm not a coach."

"You were the quarterback for the first team from Devil's Vale to win state. What else do they need?" His eyes shot up and met mine. "You have a better plan?"

"Not sure if I'm going to have much extra time. That house is a wreck."

"Fine." Dad's expression said it was anything other than fine. "But I'll be talking with Rick too. You're the best football player that ever came out of this town. I can't even tell you the number of people who've said something about that to me. The high school would be lucky to have you."

He took a long draw off his coffee cup, signaling the discussion was settled. Closed. His idea won.

∽◌

My truck shook, rattled, and bounced over the dirt path separating my house from Kate's. I was going to be lucky if I didn't need a new axel by the end of the month. Getting the holes repaired hadn't been on the almost endless to-do list, but it should have been. I might just throw that one in for free. Filling in the potholes would be cheaper than replacing the truck's whole suspension system. It might have almost ninety thousand miles on it, but my truck and I had been through a lot. I wasn't ready to trade it in for a new one. The fact that my dad said the dilapidated *thing* parked in the driveway was an embarrassment was just a bonus.

Kate's house was in such a state of disrepair that even the most dedicated renovator would probably have second thoughts about taking it on. Hell, I'd had second, third, and fourth thoughts. Gramps might have paid for half the town, but I doubted he counted on me rebuilding any house—especially one as significant as the Polk House. The thought of a Waters doing any kind of manual labor that didn't involve horses was an insult to the family name. Why had Kate insisted that I do it?

Why had I agreed?

I thudded my head against the driver's seat. I knew why I'd agreed. I was still stinging from the letter from medical school and wasn't thinking things through. Dad had sold me on a you-have-to-come-home sob story about Mom being in worse shape than she let on, but she'd seemed plenty healthy just this morning. Hell, she'd probably outlive her doctor.

Instead of being desperate to stay here, I should have taken it as a cosmic sign for me to leave this place. Devil's Vale was a black hole—maybe worse. Every time it looked like I was going to get out of its grip, something took hold of my ankle and dragged me back.

Not again.

After I finished at Kate's, I was done with this place. Max had gotten out. Screw Waters family loyalty. I was escaping too.

One more bump that threatened to take off a hubcap, and I made it onto the almost smooth gravel driveway. Since thin beads of sweat were already forming on my upper lip, I steered under the oak tree that dominated the front yard before throwing the truck into park. Seeing the pile of fresh lumber stacked just to the side of the covered porch made me breathe a sigh of relief. I could start working outside. No need to tangle with Reese this early in the morning.

I reached for my tool belt in the passenger seat before sliding out from behind the wheel. Almost as if she'd read my mind and decided to do the exact opposite of what I wanted, Reese appeared on the front porch. If I'd been drinking coffee, I would have choked.

Her t-shirt and jeans today should have been illegal. Or at least it should have been illegal to look like she did this early in the morning.

Reese's white t-shirt looked like something she'd pulled out of a multi-pack. But I'd never seen one that fit like that in my life. Of course, the local girls all tried to out-designer-clothes each other in high school. And the girls who hung around me at college were the sorority variety. Plain white t-shirts probably broke dress code somewhere.

But they shouldn't, at least not if they could emphasize curves like Reese's did. Her jeans might have been worn, but they were tight exactly where they should be. Not so tight that I wondered how she could sit down. Nothing on the pockets suggested they were overpriced designer ones like Shelby wore. The faded area at the curve of her ass looked like it was worn to almost perfect broken-in softness, and it was everything I could do to avoid marching up to her and testing my theory.

"You're early." Her cool-as-ice tone pulled me out of my fantasy.

"It's going to be hot out today." I figured that much should have been obvious, given her state of dress. There was no oversized flannel shirt today, but I wasn't complaining. "Thought I'd get an early start."

"You might want to tell your crew that some people like to sleep past 4:30." She snapped again, giving the pile of lumber a death-glare so hot I was surprised it didn't ignite.

87

"Sorry about that." I took my time walking the short distance between the house and the truck. I'd only seen apologetic-Reese and tired-Reese before. Overtired-and-pissed-off-Reese was a force to be reckoned with, but I wasn't sure if I'd had enough coffee to deal with her this morning. I hitched my thumb toward the delivery. "They're not my guys. I'd just ordered the wood. I didn't tell them when to drop it off."

"It almost scared me to death."

I had to work not to laugh at that one. Last night she'd practically dragged me up the stairs after her when we were trying to figure out what we'd heard above us. A stranger in the house didn't bother her, but a loud noise was another story. I'd have to file that one away for later because now I got a good look at her face.

She looked like hell.

Shelby would probably say whatever Reese had done with her hair was a messy bun, but calling it a bun at all was being generous. She must have piled that chocolate-brown hair on top of her head while was still wet. Now about half of it was making a break for it.

I'd seen guys on the team on their third hangover of the week with lighter circles under her eyes than she had this morning. Did she not believe in sleep? Or did she just not sleep well? Now I felt a hint of remorse at the delivery guys waking her up. I probably should have warned them that someone was staying at Kate's house now.

Was it Kate's house anymore? Judging by all the work she had to do inside, she wasn't going to be done any sooner than I was. If Reese was going to be living here a month, I might as well think of the house as hers.

"I thought I'd get started on your porch this morning."

"I figured as much, given the pile of lumber." She stabbed a finger through the air at the offending delivery before diving back into her bag. "I know they're in here somewhere." Her words came out through gritted teeth as she turned away from me to face the front door.

"Do you need some help?" I approached Reese with the same amount of caution that I used when Shelby's horse got spooked by a lightning storm.

"No," she snapped, still digging.

I waited. And waited. And worked hard not to ask again, but curiosity finally got the better of me. "Are you sure?"

"I'm fine."

I'd learned through the years that *I'm fine* typically meant I was supposed to read a girl's mind. At least that's how Shelby worked. "Did you lose something?"

Her shoulders tensed, and her free hand curled into a tight fist. She shook her bag so hard I was surprised nothing inside it broke. "I've got it. You can get to work. I don't need any help."

"It seems like you do."

Reese huffed so violently that a cobweb trembled along the doorframe. "I just can't find my keys." Her words were clipped and pointed.

"These keys?" I reached around her, trying to ignore the heat washing off her. I plucked the keys from the hand with a death-grip on her bag. She muttered a phrase I was surprised she knew under her breath. Shelby wouldn't survive if Mom heard her saying that one. I tried to disguise a laugh as a cough.

It didn't work.

"You think this is funny?"

"I'm trying really hard not to."

"At least you're honest." Her head turned in my direction, and she gave a ghost of a smile. She rolled her eyes, and I struggled to look away. Doe eyes had always been my weakness, and hers were some of the most deadly I'd ever seen. "I'm sorry for snapping this morning. I just didn't sleep well. And..."

"No apology necessary." I held up my palms in surrender. "It's hard being in an unfamiliar house—lots of noises, bed's different than what you're used to. It happens."

"Thank you. I should get to work now. Inventory isn't going to do itself." Reese gave a half-nod, adjusting her shoulder strap with one hand and waving with the other. She wrinkled her nose, showing off a sprinkling of freckles against her olive skin. "But I wish it would."

Chapter Seven

Reese

I toed off my worn combat boots inside the front door of Kate's house, tossing my head in an attempt to try to shake off the too-negative-for-a-Friday lonely vibe trying to settle over me. Why did I think Colton would be working this late? Yes, he'd still been hammering away on my porch each night when I got home this past week, but I shouldn't have expected him to still be here. After all, it was Friday night. The idea he'd have something better to do than sanding wood wasn't shocking.

What was I doing? Trying to see just how depressed I could make myself? I thrust my fingers in my hair, giving it a violent toss. Surely there was a bright side somewhere. I glanced out the picture window to study the deck. As far as I could tell, Colton had finished.

One thing checked off the to-do list. We should break out the champagne. Nope. Colton and I...weren't a *we*—no matter what my subconscious seemed to think. He was the handyman Kate had hired when she'd expected to be here to supervise him. If he weren't being paid to be here every day, I wouldn't even see him.

Still, I had to hand it to Kate—a sliver of suspicion crept into my thoughts—it was as almost as if she'd known exactly what she was doing in telling Colton what day to start, paying him in advance, and making sure the lawyer's office knew she'd hired him. But I was reaching.

I pushed back the string of thoughts I was trying to have. Kate wasn't psychic. That wasn't one of the family gifts. She'd had no way to know that death was about to meet her on her doorstep.

Her house needed repairs. Colton needed a job. Match made in heaven.

I did have to admit that having him here made things a lot less lonely. With him here just about every day when I got home, it was almost like I had a friend in town. Today my friend apparently had better things to do.

My phone buzzed in my pocket, and I just ignored it. Only one person ever called me. The last voicemail from my mother asked if I'd be done here by Monday. If I'd answered that call, I'd likely have dropped it or said something I'd later regret.

I turned and began to make my way into the kitchen. Then I rounded the corner and took in the sheer number of boxes, bags, and piles just in the den. Had there always been this many? A tiny voice whispered into my thoughts that they must be breeding.

Monday? Maybe the first Monday in December.

Reality settled over me. I'd be lucky if I could just make it through this room before July. Unless half the boxes were simply filled with trash, it would take hours just to cover the boxes flanking the fireplace. On the drive back to the house, I'd looked forward to treating myself to the bag of brownies Mabel had pushed into my hands after lunch at Mugs. She took the whole neighborly thing very seriously. When I paid my bill, she pronounced me too thin and told me to wait. With a cookie in one hand and the bag of brownies in the other hand, I left the bakery in a far better mood than when I'd walked in.

Maybe chocolate was the answer. I'd made a deal with myself: work hard at the shop, and I could have chocolate tonight. After looking at the enormity of the task facing me, I just wasn't hungry anymore.

I wandered into the kitchen since it was one of the only areas free from panic attack-inducing piles of stuff. I dropped into what had become my traditional chair and crossed my legs, resting my right ankle atop my left knee.

Franklin hopped onto the kitchen counter, purring a reminder that he hadn't eaten yet. I might have lost my appetite, but he hadn't been affected. I stood again to answer his summons. My back had stiffened during the few minutes I was seated. I let out a long breath and ignored just how out of shape I'd gotten. I hobbled to the plastic bin of cat food on the counter. Franklin's eyes followed my every movement, and he let out a cat-sniff that sounded too much like a cat-laugh. "If you're laughing, you're going to be feeding yourself tomorrow morning."

I poured the multicolored kibble into the bowl, hoping that it might inspire an idea for what I wanted for dinner. That was the problem with anticipating that Colton would still be here. So far, he'd managed to procure some type of local delicacy every night. Sure, he'd brought cheeseburgers twice, but they were the best cheeseburgers I'd ever had. I didn't mind. But tonight nothing made my stomach rumble, much less my mouth water.

Franklin gobbled his food like he hadn't eaten for a week. "You're welcome."

I scratched his head with my big toe before turning to climb the stairs. As long as I was on my feet, I might as well go upstairs and change into more comfortable clothes.

I'd just made it to the bottom step when I thought I heard something shuffling on the porch. Since Franklin turned toward the door, his mouth still filled with half-chewed cat food, I wasn't imagining it. If the ghost decided to move outside, I was seriously going to chuck something at

93

the wall. I wasn't up to another night of hide-and-seek when I never won.

A knock sounded at the door.

That was new.

The knocking happened again, louder this time. Franklin mewed and cocked his head to the side before blinking at me like he was asking if I wasn't going to check to see who was at the door.

"Okay." I glared at the cat, limped to the door, and began to turn the knob. "I'll answer the door, but you're going to see..."

But I wasn't sure what Franklin was going to see. The almost-intoxicating scent of hot pizza drifted through the door first. Then I noticed who was holding it. Colton stood in the doorway, his hair I've-been-working-all-day messy. Just a hint of stubble colored his jaw. His grin was bright enough to light the whole front porch.

The sleeves of his t-shirt strained against the bulging muscles in his upper arm. How much could he bench press? I could just faintly make out well-defined abs through the almost-see-through white fabric.

He cleared his throat, eyes alight with amusement. He gestured toward the doorway with the pizza box. "Can I come in? Not that I mind that you seem to be...distracted. But the pizza's going to get cold."

Heated rush to my face. How long had I been standing here staring at him like I was in a trance or something?

"You brought pizza?" Awesome recovery. I wanted to pound my head against the wall. "I didn't know there was a pizza place in town."

"There's not." Colton caught the edge of the door with his heel before reaching behind him to grab a paper bag. "I drove out to Albany."

"Albany?" My voice cracked in surprise. Also less-than-impressive. I was getting my flirt on tonight. What was I even thinking? I wasn't flirting. This was Colton—the handyman, the guy I'd be leaving at the end of the month, the guy who'd just driven an hour for pizza.

"You said you wanted pizza the other night. They don't exactly deliver around here." Then he walked past me, and I got a good look at the back of his jeans.

"Did I?"

"Pretty sure." He turned and looked over his shoulder, shooting a teasing grin that practically made me melt on the spot. "You were cursing the town at the time. You used the phrase 'doesn't even have a decent pizza place,' so I figured you might not know about Gordo's."

"Can't say as I've heard about it." I struggled to speak as the scent of melted mozzarella blended with an almost intoxicating amount of oregano and filled the air.

"If you don't want it, I can take it with me. I can probably find someone to share it with."

"No." My stomach rumbled and answered for me. "Pizza sounds great."

"I thought it might take some of the sting out of being stuck out here." He plopped the pizza box on the counter before turning and reaching into the cabinet for plates. With the way he knew where everything was stored in the kitchen, it was clear he was spending too much time here. After all, he could find things faster than I could.

A not-distant-enough metallic peal made me jump, and I dropped the stack of napkins I'd just pulled from the pantry.

"Seven o'clock." He turned to wink at me. "You'll get used to them."

"I'm not so sure about that."

"What? No church bells where you come from?" He stooped down and scooped up the last few napkins that had managed to sail to a stop at his feet.

"We have church bells." *Did we?* "They just don't ring quite this often." Colton started humming along with the bells. "Is that a real song?"

His eyes were filled with laughter he was too polite to voice. "It's a hymn. *Be Still My Soul.* Y'all aren't exactly church people back home?"

I bit my lip, trying to decide the most dignified response. "Church doesn't exactly go along with our line of work."

"And that is?"

Awesome, Everett. Got yourself into that one. "We run a ghost tour company." Colton would have been a great poker player. He didn't even flinch. "A little bit of history. A lot of stories to keep people awake at night."

"You get plenty of history around here." Something dark leaked into his voice, and a momentary pall settled over the room. He cleared his throat and gave his head a shake. "Pizza. Don't want it to get cold."

As he pulled the largest dinner plates down from the middle cabinet, his biceps bulged, reminding me this was also Colton, the guy who looked like he lived at the gym. I was a goner. But I'd also seen the way he looked at me. I'd seen guys more into their math teachers. His obvious *not interested* signals came across loud and clear.

"You drove into Albany?" I tried the question again. Better. No awkward screech.

"Of course. We're celebrating." He placed the bag on the countertop, and I tried to ignore the fact that was exactly where Franklin had been standing ten minutes ago. At least he set the pizza box off to the side. After reaching into the grocery sack, he pulled out a six-pack of beer.

I hoped I didn't look too shocked. I couldn't think of the last time a guy bought me a beer. Colton cleared his throat, and I realized he'd been staring at me.

Maybe now would be a good time for a game of ghostly hide-and-seek. Either that or the floor could open up and swallow me. I didn't care. Anything to get away from the I'm-trying-not-to-laugh expression on Colton's face. I fought through it.

"Celebrating. Is it your birthday?"

He backed away from the counter and started to rummage through the cabinets, victoriously pulling out a stack of paper plates on the second try. Either he'd spent more time here this week than I realized or he'd hung out with Kate in the past. I was going to hope he was just a quick learner.

"Nope, we have two things. First, you've been here a week." I wasn't sure if that counted as something to celebrate, but I didn't interrupt. "And I finished the porch."

"I knew it looked great." I limped to the window, glad that he was still selecting his slice of pizza. "It looks better than great, honestly. I've seen a lot of restoration projects over the years. If I didn't know you were the one working on it, I wouldn't be able to tell it hadn't been done by a professional."

He gave a soundless laugh, enhanced by a smirk. "I guess I'll take that as a compliment."

"It is. I mean it."

Glass tinkled as he picked two bottles up with one hand. He'd prepared two plates, and they were balanced on his outstretched arm. At some point, he'd been a waiter in the past.

"You want to grab some napkins?" He nodded back toward the roll of paper towels we'd been using as makeshift napkins during the week.

"What are we doing?"

"Eating on the porch. Didn't you hear me setting up the chairs?"

That explained the shuffling noise. "We're eating outside?"

"Something wrong with that?"

I quickly shook my head. "Not really. I just hadn't thought of it."

"A porch that big was built to be enjoyed." He paused next to the doorway. "I thought we'd take the opportunity while you're still here."

A weight dropped into the pit of my stomach. During our conversation, I'd forgotten that I didn't live here. Talking with him felt so easy. It seemed natural to be here.

"Come on out before the cheese gets cold."

"You go on out. I'll be right there." Now my ankle wasn't just sore. It had stiffened from not using it. I was glad that Colton pulled the door closed behind him so he didn't have to watch me struggle just to get to the kitchen and back. When I finally made it to the empty folding chair on

98

the porch, he seemed too preoccupied to notice my arrival. He sat, taking a long draw off the beer bottle, staring at something that only he could apparently see.

"What do you think?"

"The porch? It looks amazing." The guy was definitely fond of compliments. I'd already told him how great it looked. Now he kept fishing?

He gave a belly laugh while biting into his pizza. The apples of his cheek plumped as he smiled, revealing that pesky dimple in the corner. He hid his mouth behind his hand as he spoke.

"Not the porch. I know it looks good. I'm the one who fixed it." His eyebrows arched suggestively then he used the hand holding his beer to point to the woods in the distance.

Tiny pinpricks of light danced in the sky.

"Fireflies?" I stared at them in wonder. "I haven't seen fireflies in ages."

"Best thing about this porch. More fireflies here than anywhere else in town. I noticed them the other night. They're one of the reasons I've been staying so late."

"They're everywhere." And they were. The whole woods out in front of the house seemed filled with them. Now that I noticed one little cluster, I focused deeper into the trees and saw another and another and another. The air was practically alive.

For the next few minutes, we sat in comfortable silence, eating pizza and watching the bugs darting around. It was hard to think of something that pretty as a bug. Studying them now, following the trails of light in the night, I understood where the idea of fairies had come from. They were definitely magical.

I wasn't sure how long we went without talking. Colton ate two slices without a word, but it didn't make me uneasy. My hands stayed cool and dry, even when I noticed he was watching me.

"So. You have anyone back home waiting for you?"

I tried not to choke on my drink. "Just my parents."

"No one else?" His head tipped to the side, and he appeared to be studying me even more intently. "Someone like you doesn't have a guy?"

I leaned to the side, placed my drink on the ground, and held a hand up in caution. I might have already had a pleasant buzz going from the beer, but I wasn't sure if I was ready to dive into the who-are-you-dating pool with Colton. "Not anymore."

"Oh, sounds recent. My apologies." His too-blue eyes widened in true shock. "I didn't know I was treading into dangerous territory." He set an empty bottle on the floor and squinted like he was trying to decide if he was going to go in for another, but he seemed to decide against it. Instead, he settled deeper into his seat, furrowing his brow. "I just thought I was making conversation. Two friends, sitting on the porch, talking—that kind of thing."

Was that what we were? Friends? I had to admit that I'd enjoyed having dinner with him each night this week, and I couldn't deny that earlier wave of disappointment when I realized he wasn't here earlier this evening. But I hadn't thought we'd crossed into friends-territory.

A strange tingling in the pit of my stomach signaled that a part of me was disappointed it wasn't more. Why was I leaning his direction? And why did I have my legs crossed exactly like he did? I shifted positions in my chair to avoid mirroring him.

No way. I wasn't going there. I was only staying in town a month. Maybe six weeks. I didn't have time for a guy, and I didn't want to start something that was destined to end so quickly.

"Didn't mean to bother you." His grimace almost disrupted the peace of the evening.

"No, I'm being an idiot." I let out a breath, skimming my fingers over my collar. That's when I was shocked to remember I was only wearing a camisole. Now one of his eyes narrowed in an unspoken question. "And I'm barely even dressed. I'm sorry. I forgot I took my hoodie off."

His eyes locked with mine, and warmth spread from deep inside and out all the way to my fingertips. The look in his eyes reminded me of someone visiting an art museum. For a flash, his eyes darted from my face to the lace lining the top of my camisole. "I'm not complaining."

"Still. I..." I stood, not sure what excuse I could come up with, and it wasn't like my camisole was revealing that much. It was thicker than some of the t-shirts I'd worn this week. But I felt uncomfortably exposed. Or maybe that was just the hunger for something other than pizza I saw in Colton's eyes. I made it exactly one step before my ankle gave out beneath me.

Colton was at my side in a flash, his hand gripping my arm, a true expression of concern on his face. "Are you all right?"

"It's nothing." I tried to wave him off, but even the slightest weight on my foot caused a stabbing pain to rocket through my ankle and up my leg. "I twisted it this morning."

"Get back in the chair." He spoke the words more like an order than a suggestion. I sat. Once I was safely settled, he grabbed the armrest with one hand and my injured leg with the other. Pulling mainly on the chair, he closed the distance between us, bringing my foot to rest on his leg. His fingers gingerly tugged my sock off. "Swelling's not too bad."

"Like I said. It's nothing. I'm clumsy. I do it all the time..." Words drifting off, I lost track of my excuses because he'd begun to massage the sensitive part of my ankle, and it felt so incredibly good it was everything I could do to keep from rolling my eyes and moaning. "That feels...really awesome."

A slow smile crawled across his face, and his voice seemed deeper than normal when he answered. "We had to study massage techniques in one of my classes at school."

"You must have gotten an A."

"B plus. The final was brutal. I had to work on a guy who must have weighed 400 pounds."

"Yikes."

"Exactly."

He shifted in his seat once and again and again. If I didn't know better, I'd have assumed a bug crawled up his jeans, but that was exactly when I realized he was trying to adjust a not-so-little problem. It might be dark out, but I could still see one thing plainly. His thumb pressed on my ankle exactly twice more before he abruptly got to his feet.

Colton cleared his throat, tugging at his jeans, but that wasn't going to solve his problem. "It's late. I probably need to be going. Need any help getting into the house?"

"No. I'll be fine." I stared at the fresh boards on the porch. I couldn't meet his eyes—not when we both knew why he suddenly needed to leave.

"I'll see you tomorrow." He nodded with a jerk and sped off the porch.

After I watched his truck peel out of the gravel driveway, I half-hopped into the house. Cleaning up the remains of our dinner on the porch would have to wait until morning. I was more unsettled now than when I'd gotten home but for a totally different reason.

Maybe I wouldn't take a hot bath.

I might need a cold one. I could throw in some ice.

Using the bannister for support, I carefully mounted both landings of stairs before I went into the bedroom and rummaged through my suitcase for my favorite yoga pants and oversized sweatshirt. It wasn't quite cold enough for the long sleeves, but every time I walked through the front door a chill settled over me. This house must have a heck of a draft somewhere.

Making my way into the bathroom, I sat the change of clothes on the vanity and paused at the medicine cabinet, remembering that I'd seen a few candles tucked away on the top shelf. One was a dusty shade of green, and the other was the color of tea with too much milk. I took a tentative sniff of each.

The green one vaguely reminded me of Thanksgiving—spices, a hint of orange... or maybe it was clove. And something else. Something stronger, almost woody. I took another sniff. Probably sage or just an old holiday candle.

I inhaled a whiff of the unlit tannish candle. This smell was very familiar. It was one of my mom's favorites. Warm and comforting, but not vanilla, despite the color. Sandalwood. She always said it helped her clear her mind and let the spirits come whisper.

I didn't need any chatter from the other side, but I wouldn't turn away help clearing my mind. Thankfully, Kate left the matches with the candles. I ran one of the wooden sticks along the side of the box, hoping they weren't too old to use. I hadn't seen any downstairs, and I didn't want to have to dig through the kitchen drawers—not tonight.

A tiny, orange flame sparked almost immediately. At least one good thing had happened today. I tried not to think about the other good thing that almost happened on the porch...because I wasn't sure if it was really a good thing or not. I felt it, and I was sure he did too. For a few minutes, a connection flamed between us. I hadn't experienced heat like that since—

I wasn't sure if I'd ever experienced anything like that. If the massage had lasted much longer, we'd have needed to come inside.

And that's why I needed a bath right now. Forget the thought that one of the bath salts might be somewhat medicinal. I needed something to take my mind off what almost happened in the porch. I shifted against the unfamiliar dampness in my jeans. My mind might not be ready for a relationship, but a part of me definitely was. Even now, my nerve endings were on fire. The slightest bit of pressure in just the right place, and I knew I'd have exploded.

Not the right kind of calming thoughts.

I turned toward the tub, concentrating on relaxing. I could light the candles, and it would be like being at a spa. If I had candles, I might as well go all the way. I picked up a glass jar of what appeared to be homemade bath salts. I didn't recognize the handwriting. Kate hadn't made it. Lemon and Peppermint. The writing was nice, almost calligraphy. I looked at the bottom of the jar. Scents and Such. Shelby's handiwork.

I poured a handful of salts into the running water before peeling off my jeans and t-shirt. The best part of a bath was allowing the water to swirl around me as the tub filled. I didn't want to miss any of it. Since the hot water heater wasn't exactly in prime shape, I never knew exactly how much hot water I was going to get.

Time to live dangerously. I tested the water with the tip of my big toe. Perfect. I slid into the ancient claw-footed tub, shivering as my back made contact with the aged porcelain. Was I so tired that the hot bath would let me drown? If so, I wished my parents luck as they tried to clean out this mess without me.

I'd hoped the combination of scents wasn't going to be too overpowering, and I was happy that the bathroom was soon filled with a very pleasant amount of steam. I wasn't sure if it was the warm water or something in the bath salts, but the tension in my muscles melted away as I let myself relax into the oversized tub.

The mirror fogged over almost instantly. I closed my eyes, surrendering to the candle-lit darkness around me. *I really should take baths more often.*

I woke with a sputter, unclear how long I'd been asleep. The almost too-hot water was now simply warm, and the redness on my legs had faded. I'd been out for a while. The candles had at least an inch of melted wax pooled along the top of each.

When I'd lit them, they'd burned brightly, but the flames had mellowed during the time I'd been in the bath. Now they each only gave out a pinprick of light, but I could still see the faintest reflection in the still-fogged over mirror.

My eyes adjusted slowly, still not in too much of a hurry to get downstairs. The only thing waiting for me was a mewing Franklin. The flickering candles drew my attention. The flames seemed to be reacting to a breeze I couldn't feel. The breeze had even followed me in here. Watching the tiny orange orbs, my eyes began to unfocus. I must have been more tired than I thought.

Because the candles were fascinating.

I'd never really watched a flame before, but these two were almost alive. They pulsed with colors and danced through shapes as though they were moving or dancing...or trying to signal me.

Candles didn't contain secret messages.

Goosebumps raised along my arms. I was going insane—too much time spent in this house alone. I stood quickly with the intent to flick on the light and blow out the candles.

And that's when I saw it.

The mirror was fogged over. But not completely fogged over. It wasn't hot enough in here for that much moisture to be on the mirror. Still, I couldn't see myself. But the letters were there as plain as anything I'd ever seen.

L-E-A-V-E

Five letters.

Five letters that came out of nowhere.

At least whoever was in the house with me was being honest, even if I did find it more than a little troubling that I hadn't even sensed them. I suddenly felt blind. Uncertain. What else had I missed?

Or maybe the question was...who?

Chapter Eight
❧

Colton

The tires on my truck skidded and struggled to make the turn into the driveway. I couldn't believe I was so distracted. What was happening to me? It wasn't like I'd never touched a girl before. Hell, I'd done a lot more than touch one.

But one brush of my skin against Reese's, and it was like a fire lit inside me, and all my thoughts headed in a decidedly southern direction. I wasn't a horny kid. And I barely even knew her. Of course, that hadn't exactly stopped me before. I was going to have to work around her...how much longer? I was going to have to start my day with a cold shower. Maybe two.

No way was I making a visit up to the house tonight. I crested the hill to turn down the path toward the cabin. Just as my summer home came into view, something as effective as a cold shower hit me, wiping any last trace of my compromised state away. The lights were on.

I had a visitor, but it wasn't the one I wanted.

My best friend was gone, moved across the country. In reality, I pretty much figured out who was inside my house before I put the truck in park. I pocketed my keys, slid down from the seat, and smoothed the front of my jeans. Using the same confident stride as if my name had just been announced over the speakers at the football field, I turned the doorknob and walked into the house.

"Hello, Dad. Didn't expect to see you down here."

"Colton." He nodded, and that was apparently the only greeting I was going to get. No explanation for the house call. He must want me to sweat a little.

An assortment of bottles and glasses were on what passed for my kitchen table. I hadn't raided the liquor store. My dad had brought his own supplies. I'd interrupted him mid-pour. I didn't want to ask if it was his first drink of the night. I knew the likely answer to that question.

The crystal decanter clinked against the tumbler. Even in profile, Dad looked threatening. While he'd never been described as overly tall, his presence was always that of someone who expected everyone else to bend to his will. Tonight was no different—even out of his traditional three-piece suit. My father's coal black eyes were fixed on the golden liquid, like a hawk surveying its prey. After pouring two fingers' worth into one glass he moved on to the second.

This was going to be one of *those* conversations.

He picked up both glasses and moved toward the unneeded fire burning in the fireplace. Overhead, the whir from the air conditioner signaled its struggle against the extra heat. The fact I was supposed to follow him went without saying. His back toward me, he held out a glass, expecting that I'd take it.

I'd rather be drinking Shiner. Or maybe a lager. Max loved a good IPA, but I'd never developed a taste for them. I preferred something I could drink straight from the bottle or even chug from a can. I wasn't into the whole whisky thing. But maybe that was just because what times spent drinking in my father's presence normally entailed. Mom hated it when either of us drank, but he ignored her lectures, just like he ignored most of everything else she said.

Offered drink, I moved to the old recliner, avoiding the cast-off sofa facing the fireplace. I knew which seat my dad would choose. The sofa was once in my father's den, and as I watched him settle into a rut that seemed perfectly shaped for him, I had to wonder how many times he'd used it for his lonely reflections in the evening.

Which lecture was it going to be today?

I ran through the list of potential arguments in my head. My dad had his favorites. Most of them revolved around some disservice I was doing to the family name. As long as I'd been a winning football player, he'd overlooked the fact I wasn't planning to come back to town. Now, though, we were about a month overdue for a good father-son spat.

It would probably have something to do with the fact that I hadn't returned Rick's phone call yet. Ignoring a message of a potential future employer was a bad decision, but ignoring one when my father called in a favor was worse.

Still, he might be ready to surprise me tonight.

He cleared his throat, revving up. "I talked with Rick today."

"Did you?"

Damn. I was hoping Dad would have picked verbally wrestling about medical school. I could fight back on that one. After all, that decision was out of my hands. Mom probably didn't even knew he'd come down here. Since the coaching job was his idea, I should have known he'd hold onto it like an angry yellow jacket. I settled back in my seat, preparing to take the first verbal blow. "How's he doing?"

"Not too well." He pursed his lips, his eyes following along as he swirled his cup. "Seems like he's still short a coach. The guy he's trying to recruit won't return his phone calls."

I didn't give the calm act thirty seconds. "He'd better get on that. Two-a-days start up soon."

Dad banged his cup on the side table loud enough to wake Mom back up at the house. "Stop screwing around. He can't hold that coaching position open any longer, waiting for you to stop pretending you're a lumberjack."

Lumberjack? How many drinks had he gone through waiting for me? I turned and looked back at the table. Damn, almost a third of the bottle of whisky was gone. "I've been busy."

"I know. And a little physical labor's not going to hurt you. You got soft back at school." He narrowed his eyes, judging me like a poker player trying to predict an opponent's next hand. "I haven't said anything about it. But if it's what's keeping you from meeting with Rick, I suggest you skip a day at work."

"And what if I don't?"

"Don't be difficult. You owe us."

"Why?"

"Rick's expecting you in his office first thing Monday." He ignored my question, since it didn't fit into his agenda for the evening. "Wear a suit."

"I didn't pack mine."

"Check your closet."

I didn't want to know how Dad knew my size or had a suit delivered. I placed my untouched drink on the table. "Suit. Interview. Got it. Are we done here?"

"Not quite. The girl at Kate's. Is that her niece? Is it Reese?"

That wasn't an expected conversation either. How did he know her name? "Excuse me?"

"I'll take that as a yes." My father turned, his eyes flashing with light from the fire. "She's one of them. A Polk."

"Technically, she's an Everett. But Kate's her aunt. Great-aunt, I think."

"You really going to talk technically with me, boy?" He shifted his glasses onto the bridge of his nose and glared at me with the intensity of a judge in an old Western. "Just need to make sure."

"Of what?" Something stirred in the pit of my stomach I didn't like, and the hair raised on the back of my neck. The expression on my father's face reminded me of when we got the phone call about Max's dad. Sure, he'd seemed adequately upset at the news one of his oldest friends had killed himself, but he also seemed like he'd been expecting the call. Just like right now. He'd asked about Reese, but he clearly already knew the answer to the question.

The amber liquid in his glass shifted in time with his bouncing knee. His finger tapped out a staccato rhythm, making me wonder if he was sending a message in Morse code. He cut his eyes at me, his pupils so large and black that I couldn't make out even a hint of their normal blue. "What's she looking for?"

"I don't think she's looking *for* anything. I'm pretty sure that she's just getting the house ready to sell. Same with the store."

"She's selling the house?" For just the span of a blink, my father's jaw dropped open before he recovered. He took a long sip at his drink to fake being calm, but I'd seen it—a flash of fear and shock. Even now, his fingers shook.

111

"Yep." Normally being condescending was his job, but it was good to switch things up a bit. Somehow, I'd ended up with the winning hand in this poker game. I damn sure I wasn't giving it up.

"But she can't." He sounded like a five-year-old pleading for a new puppy.

"You're probably going to need to talk with her parents about that."

"This isn't right. That house... She's one of them." My dad skimmed the outside of his glass with his thumb. Shaking his head, he muttered something unintelligible under his breath, as if he'd forgotten I was even in the room.

I sat and watched him, waiting, but he'd moved on in the conversation without me. "Dad? We done here?"

"We're done."

I swallowed the last of the whisky in one gulp and saluted him with the empty tumbler, gesturing toward the door. "You have a good night now."

He took the hint, standing up before leaving his glass. The air in the room seemed to have cooled while we'd been talking. I almost appreciated the fire's warmth. There was a definite chill filled the air, despite it being the middle of summer.

Did it have something to do with our conversation or the freaked out expression on my father's face? I'd seen my dad drunk too many times to count. By the time I was five, I could recognize the signs of when it was dangerous to ask him a question. Now, though, his eyes were colored with genuine fear.

Without giving the collection of bottles on the table a second look, he took the first few steps toward the door. At first, I thought he was going to leave without saying anything else. He was in his own world, whispering things that sounded like *fix it* and *not the plan*. I must have been off on my guess about how much he'd had to drink tonight. If he'd been doing anything other than walking to the house, I'd have needed to take his keys away.

His hand hovered just above the doorknob, and he froze. "Kate hired you to fix her house."

"Yeah."

"So you'll be seeing more of the Polk girl."

"Reese." I corrected him. "Her name's Reese."

"Doesn't matter. One's the same as the other."

His head shook, giving the impression he was arguing with someone speaking inside his head. I was just about to argue that Reese wasn't just anyone when he stared at me with an intensity that almost burned.

"She can't sell that house. Not yet." His words rang with sober clarity. "Whatever it takes. That house has to stay in the Polk family."

Chapter Nine

ରଚ

Reese

Twenty flattened boxes lay piled along the side of the room next to the hearth without being too close to the fireplace. Six hours' work had generated ten trash bags, two smaller boxes of whatnots to take to antique store, a handful of items to research on the computer, and a backache that would take most of a bottle of painkillers to temper.

Maybe saving working on the house for a Saturday morning treat had been a bad idea. The real treat would be moving back home. Before I tossed my bag in the truck, my mom had hinted that this was something good in disguise.

I wasn't fooling myself.

Nothing waited for me back home. Nothing other than the tours and our shop. But the familiar wasn't too bad, even if I didn't have anyone to share it with.

Nope. I practically jumped to my feet, and the pain shooting down my leg almost stabbed some sense into me. I wasn't wandering down that road. Gloomy Reese had stayed back in New Orleans.

I placed my hands on the center of my back, slowly twisting to the side. At this rate, I'd have about a third of the living room cleared by Sunday. While it hadn't looked like it at first glance, most of Kate's collection seemed to be in here. I might just win the battle.

I reached down and picked up my water bottle off the floor. After unscrewing it, I took a long drink and almost choked. I'd let the water get hot. This damn house varied in temperature from sub-zero to almost-inferno. Today was definitely set to *oven*.

Which box was my next victim?

"Eeny, meeny..." I tapped my finger in midair, pointing between two stacks almost the same height, trying not to laugh when I noticed Franklin sitting on the bookshelf to my left and his tail mirrored the movements of my hand. His tail stopped before I'd finished the rhyme. "Trying to help me decide?"

I took a step toward the one his tail had chosen, tugged my scissors out of my pocket, and reached to puncture the tape. But it crumbled at the first contact with my fingertips. This had to be one of the first boxes Kate had packed.

A metallic clatter followed by a muffled string of words that ended in something that sounded like *shit muffins* rang out from the kitchen. Shit muffins? That couldn't have been what Colton said. Unless it was some kind of frat-boy code.

I had to hand it to him. After our awkward encounter last night, I wasn't sure if I'd ever see him again, especially since he'd mentioned that dude named Bud during one of our earliest conversations. I kind of figured Bud would show up today.

But I was wrong.

When I'd stepped out of the shower this morning, his truck had already been parked in front of the house. By the time I'd made it down the stairs, all traces of pizza and beer had been swept from the porch, just like they'd never happened.

And he was treating me the very same way.

Colton nodded, explained that he was ready to start work on the kitchen, and his head disappeared beneath the sink. Apart from the occasional bang, clank, or door opening, I might not have known he was in the house.

Last night had been a mistake. His actions today proved it. Until this very minute, I hadn't even heard a word from him...not even a whistle. What kind of handyman doesn't even hum while he's fixing something?

Then I heard the sound of water, and the time for asking myself pointless questions was over. I scurried into the room, almost taking myself out on the river that now trailed over the linoleum.

"What did you do?"

"Nothing. It just went insane." Colton was leaning over the sink, rubbing the back of his head with one hand while pounding the lever of the sink with the other fist. His cheeks burned tomato-red as he reached in the bowl of the sink and pulled out the stopper before dropping back to his knees.

Splashy paw-steps announced Franklin's arrival, but he only tried to sit once before jumping onto the kitchen table. I would have scolded him for his seat choice, if I didn't know how much he hated water. Right now, his options for dry footing were limited.

"Got it." His words were victorious as the sound of the water stopped.

I stared down at my feet. The damage wasn't as bad as I'd originally thought. It hadn't risen above the lip of the floor separating the living room from the kitchen. Not really too much worse than overturning a too-full mop bucket, really.

"Colt—" I only got half the word out before it felt like someone dropped a hammer onto the center of my head.

"I'm pretty sure you were about to ask me what I did to flood the kitchen." Colton half-stood, half-knelt next to me with his hands pressed to his knees. Based on the way his forehead was crinkled and the fact that it seemed like I was wet from the back of my head down to my socks, something far worse than a flooded kitchen had just gone wrong.

"Something like that." I started to sit up, but he moved so fast, it was like he'd shifted into fast forward. He pressed a hand to my shoulder and pushed me back down against the couch.

That's when I realized I was sprawled on the couch in Kate's office. Since I didn't remember walking in here...I glanced at Colton's shirt. Sure enough, a wet spot roughly the size of me stood out on his chest. He'd carried me in here. Awesome. This couch was getting far too much use as a recovery room.

He pushed my feet out of the way and took a seat on the far end of the couch. Grimacing, he scratched absently at the back of his neck. "No idea. One second I was hammering the new floor of the cabinet in place and the next, water was pouring out of the sink. I'd just about gotten it turned off when I heard something thud." His eyes fixed on mine, and he gave a grin that looked like forced amusement. "That would be when you hit the floor. Did you slip?"

"No." My head was starting to pound in time with my pulse. "I had a headache."

"A headache did that?"

"Apparently."

"Is that common for you? I mean, your parents shouldn't have sent you here alone. That's not safe."

"No." I sat up, despite his repeated attempt to prevent me from becoming vertical. "Never."

"Well, you freaked me out." His eyes blinked faster than my pulse right now, and my heart seemed to be pounding at record speed. I tried to convince myself that it had nothing to do with his proximity to me and everything to do with the fact I'd just passed out...but even I wasn't buying what I was selling. "You've been working long hours. Maybe you should take it easy this afternoon. Why don't you just chill tonight? Watch some TV or something."

I hadn't been overdoing it. I'd worked longer hours than this before. When we were restoring one of the missions in south Texas during my junior year, the team from my school worked eighteen-hour days for almost three weeks straight during the hottest June on record. I wasn't just tired.

At least I wasn't that tired.

But I didn't want to tell him a headache made me pass out. Colton already wore a freaked-out expression that suggested he'd never have cut it in medical school—not unless they liked their residents' faces to match the whiteness of the sheets. Dude would probably never leave me alone again...although that wasn't such a bad thought.

"Maybe you're right. I've been working long days. And it's hot. I'm not used to the humidity here." In New Orleans it was worse. Still, if he could pretend I hadn't freaked him out, I could act like he'd guessed right. "I'll take it easy. Read a book or something. Maybe Kate has some DVDs that aren't black and white."

"And you promise to eat something?"

"I can manage. I actually do know how to cook." And then I started thinking about the kitchen again. "Why were you running water in the sink anyway?"

"I wasn't." He tilted his head, doing a decent impression of a doctor doing an exam. "I already told you that. Remember?"

I blinked.

"Then how did the water turn on?"

"Maybe your cat bumped the lever. It's kind of loose. That's on my to-do list."

"Maybe." I nodded in agreement, but I couldn't shake the thought I was missing something. It buzzed around me like a moth circling a security light. "Franklin likes to hang out in the kitchen."

"I'd better go." A long sigh escaped his lips. Colton tentatively reached out and almost brushed my cheek. His eyes studied the floor, and he bit down on the corner of his lip. "I can stay tonight. In case you have any more trouble."

"I'll be fine." I nodded, forcing my voice to sound more confident that I felt.

"No more work tonight."

"I'll be good. I won't even get off the couch. Total girl's night. I'll even find some chocolates somewhere."

"You sure?"

"Positive."

He grimaced as he seemed to swallow down an attempt at prolonging the discussion. Worry lurked in the way the corners of his eyes crinkled. "Because I can drive into town and get burgers. You haven't tried the green chile ones yet."

"If I try any more burgers, I won't be able to wear any of the clothes I brought with me. I can't afford to buy new ones—not if I'm paying for grad school next semester." I gave what I hoped was a firm but playful shove.

"Hand me your phone."

"Why?"

"Just give me the phone." He extended his hand like it wasn't a request.

I pulled my phone from my pocket and dropped it into his palm. Colton tapped a few keys before giving it back to me. "There. You have my number. If you need anything, and I mean anything, just give me a call."

"Thanks. I'm not gonna need it."

"Just humor me."

"Sure. I promise."

He alternated his weight between his feet, appearing indecisive. I almost thought he was going to stay. I almost let him. Just when I opened my mouth to agree, he turned toward the door. "Good night, Reese. Be careful."

ß

Aunt Kate didn't have any bon bons hidden in the kitchen. The house also didn't have cable. And I'd hit my *you've used seventy-five percent of your data plan* warning yesterday. If I used it all, my parents would turn my phone off completely. So I was stuck staring at the ceiling.

After two hours, I'd memorized the cobweb-like pattern of cracks in the ceiling. This was ridiculous. My head felt fine. I felt fine. I was itching to get back to work.

Thankful that Colton had decided to leave, since I was pretty sure he'd send me upstairs if he saw me step one foot into the living room, I walked to the box where I'd left off. The scissors still sat on top of the half-opened box. I flipped the cardboard lips open, revealing a cluster of wadded-up newspapers at least three inches deep. Kate wanted to make sure nothing in this box was damaged.

I hit a layer of tissue paper followed by bubble wrap. I put the wrappings to the side with a smile. I'd save it for de-stressing later. Glancing around at just how much I still had to do, and I knew I'd need some bubble-popping relief later. Possibly later tonight.

Finally, I got the first glimpse at what Kate had been so careful to preserve, and I had fight back a laugh. A tiny gift-wrapped box, complete with a glinting metallic bow sat on top of a heavy, leather photo album. I pulled the box out first, noticing a gift tag written in Kate's careful script. *Reese.*

I juggled it between my hands, not sure what to do. Obviously, it was meant for me. But should I just open it? Based on conversations I'd overheard between my parents, Kate had seemed a little absentminded in her last few years. Judging by the condition of the house, what my mom defined as *a little* might be questionable.

This must have been intended as a gift. A heavy feeling settled in my chest as I wondered just how long she probably searched for this box after accidentally packing it. I flicked the bow with the nail of my index finger.

This was mine.

Or at least it was supposed to be mine. After all, the gift tag was addressed to me. My birthday was next month.

"Happy early birthday to me." I whispered, glancing at Franklin who'd joined me in the room. I ripped the paper. Mom would have been displeased, but after sifting through too many houses where people had saved way too much stuff, I wasn't into the whole saving-the-wrapping-paper thing.

Once the paper was gone, I was holding a plain white box in my hand. I lifted the lid, revealing the same kind of cottony square I typically found in a jewelry box, which made sense when I pulled it out.

A black bracelet sat on another square of cotton.

Not just a plain black bracelet.

A series of black beads linked by a gold chain.

I carefully removed it from the box. I couldn't tell how old it was, since I'd never seen anything like it. The beads were flecked with crimson veins and deeper black crystals that looked like black marble. Thirteen beads were between the clasp and a teardrop cameo with thirteen beads on the other side of the charm.

It wasn't exactly my taste. I didn't wear a ton of black. But it looked vintage, and I thought the tourists might like it when I led the ghost tours. Maybe that's what Kate had in mind when she'd bought it. After all, it did have a certain gothic quality to it. Since I didn't have anyone to help me with the clasp—well, anyone other than Franklin—I squeezed my fingers together and slid it over my hand.

The bracelet was heavy. I'd hate to pick up a brick of whatever stone the beads were made from, but it was pretty. I liked the way the deeper black flecks seemed to pick up the light from the overhead lamp. And the cameo wasn't really too big. It wouldn't get in the way. Leaving it on, I turned my attention back to the box and removed the photo album.

The album was old, likely from the turn of the century, if not earlier. The leather had a few minor age cracks, but nothing that really compromised it too much. Breathing in the scent, I was reminded of an old saddle. The tips of my fingers tingled when I reached for the cover. Careful to notice even the slightest bit of resistance, I opened to the first page. Handwriting I didn't recognize spelled out the word *Polk*. At least I wasn't going to have to do much research before putting it in the keep pile. Mom would want this piece of family history.

Part of me wanted to put the book to the side to keep my momentum going, but another part of me was curious about just who made up my family. Apart from Kate and my grandparents, I wasn't sure if I'd ever seen a photograph of any of my ancestors.

Peeling back the cover page, I revealed the first photograph and almost dropped the book. It was like looking at a mirror. The young woman almost glaring from the page could have easily been my sister, if not my twin. Her eyes burned at whoever was taking the picture. I'd have hated to be on the receiving end of that glare.

She might look like me, but I hoped I'd never stared at anyone with that degree of hatred. Studying her face, I realized she couldn't have been much older than I was now. No wrinkles lined her face, and she was still almost stick-thin. Her hands were folded atop her knee, and I noticed something else familiar. She was wearing my bracelet.

Or I guessed I was wearing hers.

Was this a family heirloom? I raised my arm, bringing the bracelet level with my eyes for closer inspection. It definitely looked like the same piece of jewelry. If it was, then it was at least a hundred years old, perhaps older.

I turned my gaze back down to the picture, noticing the handwriting for the first time. I hated it when people wrote on pictures. I'd lost count of how many valuable photos had been destroyed by ink leaking into fragile paper. But since this was the only way I'd figure out who my apparent doppelganger was, I guessed I'd have to give my relative a pass on this one.

Annabelle Polk

1844 – 1865

Annabelle Polk? Her name didn't ring any bells. Despite being in the business of preserving history, my family hand never excelled at passing along information about our own ancestors beyond the whole some-of-them-could-see-ghosts thing. I typically didn't mind not being hung up on the past. Tonight I'd have been open to sharing a few more details.

I flipped through the rest of the album, hoping for a note, a letter, even a recipe card that might give me a hint about who this Annabelle was.

Nothing.

Just more photographs. She wasn't in a single one. Now I really did have a headache. It wasn't every day I discovered an ancestor who could have easily been my identical twin. I carefully closed the timeworn album and placed it on the floor next to me.

I stared down at the face peeking through the cutout cover—the face that was mine while it still wasn't. "Annabelle Polk, looks like you're going to make me take a trip to the historical society."

ß

The door to the library swung shut behind me, and I adjusted the stack of books in my arms. I had to admit, the librarian hadn't batted an eye when I asked for directions to the Civil War section. She probably got that a lot this time of year.

I didn't get an odd look until I said I was doing research on the Polk family. That little mention drew a quick fluttering of the woman's wrinkled eyelids followed by a squint so intense a little kid would have run in fear.

I wasn't a little kid, but I still didn't linger in the library any longer than necessary—not when I kept hearing the creaks and pops of the wooden floor that hinted that I was being followed while doing my research. Since I didn't really know what I was looking for, I'd checked out a sampling of books from the right era. The people around here believed in preserving history. I'd never seen so many books centered on one small town.

I dumped the books in my truck before strolling to the center of the square.

I loved town squares. This one was actually nicer than most. I had to hand it to the residents of Devil's Vale—they knew their history. From the colors on the trim of the buildings to the cast-iron lanterns, these buildings probably looked like they did back at the turn of the century.

With Mrs. Carter at the helm of the Preservation Society, I didn't know why I expected anything less.

With the sun high overhead, I retreated to the shade of the large oak tree, rimmed by a white picket fence. This tree was so old that it probably remembered before the town was even settled. I ran my hand over the branch, not sure why it attracted my attention. It was just a branch on an oak tree. Sturdy, yes. Bigger than a baseball bat probably, but still, other than the unusually smooth section in almost the exact middle, nothing really spectacular.

"I see you found the hangin' tree," a voice called out from behind me.

"The what?" I turned to face an unfamiliar man leaning on the grille of his Cadillac. One foot rested on the bumper just to the side of the LAW-YER license plate. His worn cowboy hat was pulled down almost over his eyes. I was surprised he could see anything, much less me standing next to a tree.

He tipped his hat back with the tip of his index finger. One side of his lips lifted in a threatening grin.

"The hangin' tree. Just what it sounds like." He pushed off from the hood and approached me. Something about the way he stared made me wonder if he was responsible for feeling like someone was watching me while I was in the library. His eyes were overly familiar, as if he'd been studying me...following my movements. "See how that branch is all nice and smooth there. Just one reason for that."

"Hanging?"

"You heard me right. Folks used to come from miles around to see one." His eyes held the sense of wonder of a child walking into Disney World for the first time. "Busiest days of the year, my daddy used to say. Ladies'd get all gussied up in their Sunday best. Little ones thought it was some kind of holiday."

Something about his speech told me he was exaggerating his accent on purpose. If his license plate wasn't a lie, he was a lawyer for pity's sake. He didn't need to be playing the country-bumpkin routine with me. Unless he had a reason.

"I suppose you've seen one." I wasn't going to let him rattle me.

"Nah. Before my time." He swatted at one of the ever-present mosquitoes buzzing his face. "Just the stories my daddy used to tell me." He blinked and his eyes narrowed. "Why are you here?"

"Just looking. Visiting the library."

"Not here." He turned and spat on the ground, completing the country-boy facade. "Here. Your folks left Devil's Vale when you were barely walking."

"I was eight." I bit back the part of the reply that I'd hardly call that barely walking. "How do you know who I am?"

"It's a small town, sweetheart. Why'd you come back?"

Something in his demeanor made me stiffen. *I thought you knew everything. Not a mind reader, are you?* "Someone needs to clean out Kate's house."

He nodded slowly, staring into the breeze. "Figured it'd be your momma. Why isn't she here?"

A tinge of suspicion tickled at the pit of my stomach. Why the twenty questions? "She couldn't make it."

"Your aunt used to be important to her. She couldn't clear time in her busy schedule? That ghost tour business really keeping her that tied down?"

"She was in a wreck. She couldn't come. Does that explain things?"

He didn't miss a beat. "I suppose so." He started walking away from me, slowly making his way back to the driver's side of his car. Just before he disappeared inside, he hesitated and looked over his shoulder. His cold, dark eyes met mine. "Next time you talk to your momma, tell her I hope her leg's better soon."

I stood there, staring at the place he'd once stood. I hadn't mentioned her leg. How had he known what happened to my mom? The chill in the pit of my stomach told me I didn't want to know.

Chapter Ten
ᢒᢙᣆ

Colton

My phone buzzed in my pocket, and I tugged it out a little too quickly, thinking it might be Reese. Another call from the office manager at my old apartment. Awesome. Just what I needed today.

No matter what either of us pretended, we both knew Reese didn't pass out from the heat. I was kicking myself for leaving at all. Now I couldn't even run by the store to check on her—at least not until after my meeting.

My phone vibrated again, and a red dot indicated I had yet another voicemail from them. Just yesterday, they'd moved on from the vague hints at me needing to return to settle things with them. The message was much more to-the-point than earlier ones. "Come clean it out by tomorrow, or you'll forfeit your security deposit."

At least they weren't beating around the bush anymore. Since the security deposit was paid with my dad's money, and he was the reason I couldn't drive back to school today, they were going to have to figure out what to do with the random pieces of furniture I'd collected through the two years I'd spent there. Dad wouldn't miss the $500. He definitely wouldn't miss it as much as he'd be angry if I skipped the meeting he'd set up with Rick.

The one o'clock follow-up interview was the whole reason I wasn't going to be able to make it out to Reese's house today. I thought I'd bombed the meet-and-greet on Monday. I'd arrived at the high school office wearing the suit my dad had ordered and walked into a conference room filled with my former teachers. The surprised expressions on their faces had likely matched my own. Rick had strode in and sat at the head of the table before things got too awkward, but they were questionable enough.

During our chat, I'd stumbled over one question after another.

Why did I want to teach?

If I'd been interested in coaching, why didn't I take an education classes?

Was I willing to commit to the school long-term?

I'd almost choked on my coffee after that one. My old history teacher had kept mumbling a word that sounded like certified and clearing her throat. The obvious shake of her head had told the rest of the table where she stood on the idea of adding me to the faculty. I couldn't blame her.

When I'd left the school, the overwhelming relief felt like my old coach had just cancelled practice on a day it was raining. No question about it—I was off the hook. No Devil's Vale High School for me.

I'd been finishing breakfast when Dad came in, glare already locked-and-loaded. He tossed a piece of paper my direction with all the specifics about my second meeting at the school, and I dropped my fork, almost cracking the china. "What's this?"

"Pretty sure you can read." He'd even listed what tie to wear—yellow with blue stripes. Overkill was just my dad's style.

I knotted my green tie phone before turning to face the mirror. My dad would say I needed a haircut. I doubted he'd ever seen my hair quite this long. And my eyes definitely didn't have an I-really-want-this-job look in them. Maybe Rick would tell me I wasn't the right guy for the job after all.

Of course he wouldn't. I bit back a laugh. He was on the city council with my dad. Around here, what council members wanted, tended to happen...just like magic. I ran my hand over my jaw. Shaving would have been a good idea too, but that would hint I wanted this job.

Damn, I needed to talk to Max. I hadn't heard from him since he'd left. I really didn't know if this was unusual for him or not. We'd never been in a situation where we needed to text each other. I couldn't think of a single day in my life where I hadn't seen him.

Not until he left for Seattle. If he hadn't sent me a single message saying his flight had landed, I'd have assumed he'd died along the way. But he was there. Busy, I guess. Too busy to answer me.

I needed Max to convince me this was a bad idea. When we'd tried to decide which coach might replace his dad, neither of us mentioned my name. I'm sure he'd find this whole situation hilarious.

But that wasn't the whole joke. Before it could be funny, he had to know I might be the new high school coach. For that to happen, he had to return my call. Hell, he could even text me. I didn't care. He'd always been the one person who understood just how insane my dad could be. And now he was gone.

"Now what's that look on your face for?" Mom stood in my doorway, head cocked to the side, looking far older than her not-quite-sixty years.

I ran my hand over the back of my neck as I thought. So far, she'd done a great job of pretending she believed I was excited about the possibility of coaching for Devil's Vale.

"I didn't hear you come in."

"I knocked." She forced a smile that didn't come close to reaching her eyes. "I saw your truck out in front and figured you'd still be here." Her eyes narrowed as she looked out the window. "Max's car is still out there too. Looks like it's gathering dust. When are you going to start driving it? Your truck looks like it would like the rest."

"I'm saving it for when Max comes back." This wasn't the best time to be talking about him, but she'd always had an uncanny knack for knowing exactly what I was thinking.

"Mind if I sit down?" Her voice had the airy quality of a runner who'd pushed too hard on the track.

"No, take your pick."

My once-tough-as-nails mother stepped into my room and made her way to the wingback chair next to my dresser. She sat down, breathing hard from just walking down from the main house. I'd been trying not to notice just how much frailer she'd gotten, even since I'd been here. I guessed both of us had been lying to each other.

"Now what's that look for?" She sounded more like Grandma than herself.

"What look?"

She raised her eyebrows, shaking her head in disappointment. "You know better than to try to pull something over on me." She squinted one eye closed and aimed a finger at my forehead. "Your dot's glowing."

"I haven't believed in my momma dot in a long time, Mom."

"Humor me." She sat back in the chair, letting her fingertips trace the edge of the trim, but her eyes didn't lose focus on mine. "And why don't you explain why you look like you're trying to decide if you need to pick out flowers for my

131

funeral arrangement all of the sudden. Do I really look that bad?"

"No." If I had a dot, it would be flashing red right now.

"Liar." A flicker of sadness washed over her eyes, but it was gone by the time she blinked. "Even I know it. I told your daddy not to tell you, but you're too smart for your own good. Chemo's not working this time."

I muttered something that would have gotten my mouth washed out with soap when I was little. This time, my mom didn't bat an eye.

"Pretty much." She smiled stoically, and she looked even more like my grandma than before. "Doctor Hume says we still have a few more good months left. Let's not waste them."

A few months?

Damn, that hit me harder than when Max told me he was moving to Seattle. I'd seen the changes in her, but I never expected...not something like this. I should have seen it. Hell, I did see it. But I'd been lying to myself just as much as I'd been lying to her.

I turned and looked at the clock. There was time. I reached to unfasten the top button of my dress shirt. "Excuse me, mom."

"What are you doing? Don't you have to be somewhere?"

I nodded. "But first, I need to shave."

ß

Rick Yancy circled his desk before coming to perch on the armrest of the chair directly to my right. I'd been in this office several times through the years, sometimes for good reasons. More often for ones that would earn a discussion with my dad that night. I never got in real trouble here. He knew with one call to my house, I'd be in more than enough trouble that night.

Mr. Yancy always waited until dinnertime to call. During my sophomore year, I'd gotten to where I hated to hear that phone ring. Dad would shoot one glare at me, and I knew I'd be lucky if I could still sit down the next day at school.

I never dreamed I'd be here, in this office, talking about a job.

"So. You're moving back to town." Mr. Yancy—Rick—held a manila folder open, and he nodded as he read the resume my dad must have sent him.

"Looks that way, yeah." I corrected myself. "Yes, it looks that way."

"You made good grades at school."

Hell yes, I did. Good grades went along with the whole planning-to-go-to-medical-school thing. "I did my best."

"Better than what I remember from the time you were here."

"I was motivated." No reason to mention my post-college plans. No reason to bring up a topic even I didn't have answers for, since no one at Augusta College of Medicine had answered a call or an e-mail so far when I'd wanted an explanation.

"I can see that. Biology. Chemistry. Anatomy. A lot of sciences."

"I like science."

"I remember. I remember." He nodded faintly. "You won the science fair your junior year. Something about sports drinks."

"Right. I'd been testing if sports drinks actually impact the ability to work out harder."

"And do they?"

I tried to remember. "It's been a few years. I don't think they did. Water worked just as well."

"Try telling that to our coaching staff." He closed the folder and placed it on the desk in front of us. "Which, I think will be easy enough to do once you join them."

And now we moved into the section of the interview when things were bound to get sticky. I had to admit, so far, things had gone more smoothly than I expected. No questions about why I was here, why I wanted the job, or why I'd be qualified without a teaching degree. Honestly, he hadn't asked many questions at all.

"You were a great player here. I saw you at the Rose Bowl in college. They wouldn't have won without your arm. And your daddy told me you volunteered at the Boys' Club?"

I volunteered there because it looked good on my medical school application. "I coached their flag football team."

"See, you even have experience." He smiled at me in a way that said he was trying to convince me I was qualified to coach, not the other way around. Something seemed off. Wrong. This wasn't an interview. Everything had already been decided.

"But I don't have a teaching degree."

He waved his hand like he was swatting at a fly. "That's easy enough. We can file the papers saying you're the most qualified for the job. With all your science classes, you'd be a great addition to the faculty there too. Just take a couple of tests in the fall, and you'll be all set. Expect a call from Ms. Jones. You remember her, right?"

"Little lady who taught Chemistry?"

"That's the one." He pushed off from the arm of the chair and started walking toward the door to his office. "She'll let you know when the team's first day back will be."

"That's it?" I hadn't even been in his office for ten minutes.

"Unless you have questions for me." He paused with his hand on the doorknob.

The only question I had for him was the one I knew he wouldn't answer: why did he and my dad want me back here so badly?

Chapter Eleven
༄༅

Reese

After a moderately productive weekend, I had to walk away from all my progress and go back to the store. If I worked hard enough, I'd be done here within a few more days, so I'd started work even earlier than last week, tossing Colton a spare key as we passed in the driveway this morning.

I'd kept up the momentum from Saturday and Sunday when I returned to the store. In the first few hours of the morning, I'd managed to finish cataloging the entirety of the collection of antique sterling silver. I had to give my great-aunt credit. She knew her antiques. I didn't have to toss out a single piece for not being authentic.

I choked back a string of curses when a knock sounded at the front window of the store, dragging me from the storeroom. I'd almost ignored it, since I was so close to being completely finished there, but whoever it was knocked with attitude. I rocked onto my toes, catching a glimpse of gray hair pulled tightly into a bun. My visitor was accustomed to getting what she wanted. And with the intensity she was still using to knock, she wasn't going away—or at least she wasn't leaving until she got in or broke the glass.

I didn't want to clean up another mess, so I answered the door. "Can I help you?"

Without waiting to be invited in, my visitor pushed past me. "I'm surprised I haven't heard from you yet."

"I have no idea what you're talking about."

"I'm Rose Carter." She shoved a pile of pamphlets into my hand. "I'm the president of the Devil's Vale Preservation Society." She spoke the title like I needed to be impressed. "I expected to hear from you about the renovations to Polk House by now."

"Still kind of at a loss here."

"I suppose Kate didn't get around to giving you my number." I let my silence announce that I was still not up to speed with whatever she and Kate must have talked about. Rose huffed through her nose like an annoyed horse. "The renovations—of your aunt's house. I'd asked her for the plans back in May, but she said she couldn't give them to me until you got here."

"Until I got here?"

"To help her plan the renovations." She looked at me like she was trying to decide if I'd been drinking on the job or if I was just this slow. "She said you were the expert, and she wouldn't make any decisions without your approval."

"She thought I was coming?"

"Knew you were coming is more like it." Now it was Mrs. Carter's turn to appear confused. Confused, but still bossy. She flipped through a tiny hard-backed journal, spinning it around to give me a look. Sure enough, that was Kate's handwriting and my cell phone number. "She told me to expect you the last week of May. You were late."

How did I explain to her that I couldn't be late when I didn't even know I was coming? "Sorry. My mom had a wreck. She was in the hospital in May."

"Oh." That cut her annoyance level back a few notches. "I didn't know. Kate didn't say anything about that. My apologies. But about the plans for the house?" She was like a dog refusing to let go of a dirty sock. "We're meeting next week. The Preservation Society needs to sign off on them if our funds will be used for part of the restoration."

I could use all the help with paying to restore the house that I could get. I glanced around the shop. If I'd known I had a deadline on the house, I would have switched where I'd started. "I have one more week working here. But then I can really focus on the house. I got a good start this weekend. I guess I can probably have them to you next Monday."

She gave a quick nod, and I wondered if she'd been a librarian in a former life. "I suppose that'll work." One eye narrowed in warning. "But make certain you have it ready by then. I'll come by the house at ten."

She turned and left before I could even agree with her. I had the strong suspicion that I wasn't really part of the decision. Whether or not I was ready for them, the Preservation Society was ready to get their hands on the house.

But why had Kate told her I was going to be here?

Something thudded on the door again. I resisted the urge to yell that if Mrs. Carter kept interrupting me, I wouldn't be able to work on her precious promised plans. I swept back toward the door, almost knocking a set of crystal candlesticks off the edge of a fake mantle before I calmed down enough to answer the door. "Did you forget something?"

I heard the low snorting laugh before I saw who delivered it.

"I see you've met Mrs. Carter." My neighboring shop owner smiled with a welcome-wagon grin. "I thought you might like to take a little break."

She jiggled a white paper bag and nodded down at a coffee carrier holding two cups. The scent of baked goods mixed with caffeinated goodness drifted through the door.

I made a mental note to ask Colton to check the weather stripping on the screen door. I unlatched the lock, pushed the door open, and beckoned my neighbor to come inside.

"Thank you..." Scarlett? Sydney?

"Shelby." Her voice had a sultry edge I'd expect to hear on a perfume commercial.

"Shelby." I repeated, hoping to drill it into my brain somehow. "It's nice of you to think of me, but I really can't."

"Nonsense." She waved my excuse away as if it were a fly. "Everyone needs a break from time to time. I know I needed to take a few minutes away from melting my wax." Her hand tucked a wavy strand of perfectly blond hair behind her ear. Sweat beaded at her hairline, and her foundation was dripping just a bit. She really did need the break. But that didn't mean I had to join her. "I hope you like chocolate."

Chocolate was my biggest weakness. Coffee came in a close second.

Put the two together, and it was like one of the *you've just inherited a million dollars from a relative you've never heard of in Nigeria* spam e-mails was actually true. Maybe I could afford a short break.

"I'm so sorry I've been so remiss in visiting. I know it can be kind of difficult to be new here. Not that I've ever been new in Devil's Vale. Waters are just like the Polks. We've always been here."

She made her way to the back of the shop like she owned the place. Before I really understood what was going on, she'd opened the cabinet over the ancient microwave and pulled down a stack of paper plates I hadn't even known was there.

"I'm not exactly a Polk. My last name's Everett." I hesitated to correct her since she'd brought coffee.

Shelby pulled one of the mint green chairs back from the ice cream table that served as the break area in the kitchen. She placed two plates down opposite each other before reaching into a drawer for a stack of napkins. Satisfied with her place setting, she set the coffee in the center of the table as she took a seat.

"Reese," she *tsked* like a teacher dealing with a recalcitrant student. "You're in the South now, sugar." She spoke the words as if she were explaining that I no longer lived in the United States. "We're a matriarchal society. Your last name may not be Polk, but that doesn't change anything. You're a Polk just as much as I'm a Waters."

Her visit took longer than a few minutes. By the time I'd finished my coffee and muffin, half the morning had passed by. I couldn't complain too much since the unexpected treat alleviated my need for lunch.

The only real problem with the little coffee break was it distracted me. I almost forgot about the unanswered question of exactly why Mrs. Carter was so convinced that Kate had been expecting me to visit. By the time I'd locked the front door behind me, I wasn't sure if the tense muscles in my neck came from the just-a-little-too-odd-for-comfort question or if I'd just lifted too many boxes onto the top shelf in the storage closet.

I was still pondering that question as I drove past Mugs, almost missing the friendly wave from the Mabel. And I was still trying to decide if I'd somehow forgotten a conversation I'd had with Kate as I closed and locked the front door of the house behind me. I'd texted my mother to ask, but I found myself still waiting to hear from her to see if she'd had a conversation with Kate she'd forgotten to discuss with me.

Too much was happening too quickly. No matter what Mom said about this just being an antique shop and Kate being just a *normal* member of the family, I was beginning to suspect that wasn't true. Or at least the rumors were true, and her house was haunted.

Those letters didn't write themselves on the bathroom mirror. More than once, Franklin had hissed at something I couldn't see. And nothing explained the random knocks and bumps in the house. Old houses creaked, but not rhythmic footsteps down the stairs.

Kate must have collected spirits just like she'd collected knick-knacks. I just couldn't see them. I didn't like the sensation of losing one of my senses. I'd never worked at this kind of disadvantage before—or at least I didn't think I had.

I cursed the fuzzy cloud that seemed ever-prevalent when I tried to remember when I lived back here. We left when I was seven. Didn't most kids remember their childhood friends? Shouldn't someone here remember me?

This was the kind of place where gray-haired old women should come up to me and tell me embarrassing stories about when I was little. Even if I didn't know them, they should have faintly remembered the brown-haired girl with pigtails who hung around Kate's shop.

Colton was only two year older than I was. He'd grown up here. Devil's Vale was even smaller back then. He didn't remember me...at all? And Shelby was my age. I didn't know her at all. One of them should have had some kind of memory, shouldn't they? Or at least I should remember them.

Damn it. The more I tried to focus, the fuzzier things got.

Chapter Twelve

Reese

The bell on the front door jangled, jarring me from my sorting. I must have forgotten to lock it. The closed sign should have told people not to come in, but I'd quickly learned that didn't always work around here.

Shelby might have dropped in again. For someone with a shop of her own, she seemed awfully interested in mine. No, this was Kate's shop, not mine. And it made sense for her to know what was going to happen with the antique store, since having it closed probably affected her business as well.

I took a sniff and didn't smell muffins, coffee, or the vaguely vanilla scent that seemed to perpetually cling to her. She'd never dropped in without snacks for reinforcement. I stood upright, brushing the layer of accumulated dirt off my hands.

It was probably Mrs. Carter. I doubted she'd let something like a closed door stand in her way.

As much as I welcomed the break, I couldn't afford it. Surely Mrs. Carter hadn't come back so soon. I'd told her I'd have the plans to her in a week, not a day. The muscles in my neck started tightening at the thought of dealing with Mrs. Devil's Grove Preservation. If they were in that much of a hurry, they should have hired an architect. They were lucky they were getting my plans for free.

I knew who it most likely wasn't. I doubted Colton would come through the door uninvited, and my stomach seemed to drop down into my feet. He was the one person I wanted to see this morning.

Things had been weird since Saturday.

He'd been all business, not staying for dinner, barely even talking to me. After the fuss he'd made about giving me his phone number and calling if I had any trouble, I thought we'd made some sort of connection beyond handyman and employer. Apparently I'd judged incorrectly.

That should have made me happy. I should have been breathing a sigh of relief because I didn't want to have to mess with any kind of romantic tangle. But I did. The more I tried to block out any thought of Colton, the more I seemed to fixate on him.

The way he smelled...leather mixed with old car and a hint of aftershave. The way he worked silently, without even a whistle or a hum. The way his eyebrow arched when he caught me looking at him. Attractive, too confident for his own good, reformed jock with no immediate career prospects—he was everything I didn't want in a guy.

Except I really wanted him.

Someone was moving out in the main store. I willed it to be Colton, even though I knew he was probably back working on my house. Not my house. Kate's house. This was *not* my new address.

My heart did a quickstep as I smoothed my wrinkled t-shirt. Maybe Colton had a question for me. I hadn't given him my cell phone number, and Kate's store phone had been shut off. My cheeks flushed as I reached for the door to the storeroom.

"Hello?" A voice laced with worry called out from the front of the store. A female voice. Definitely not Colton. I bit back a wave of disappointment.

Great work, Reese. Keep this up, and someone would be able to clean the whole place out while I'm still in the storeroom.

"Sorry," I called out, wiping my hands again on the dirty fronts of my jeans, not sure if I was removing dust or just adding to it. There must have been a cobweb mixed in with some of the dust...or glue. This stuff just wouldn't come off. I glanced down at my palms. Clean enough. "I'll be right with you."

I opened the door to the store room, and a headache hit me as soon as I walked through to the store. My steps faltered under its intensity. For a moment, the room darkened to almost black, and I stumbled into a curio cabinet. My bracelet caught on something, and I reached out blindly to untangle it. I didn't even remember putting it on this morning. I should have taken it off. If I'd broken what must be a family heirloom, I wouldn't forgive myself. Still, if I took it off now, I'd probably put it down and lose it amid the rest of the knick-knacks. I gave the cameo a tug, and it didn't seem any worse for wear.

My eyesight gradually returned, and I hoped whoever was in the shop wasn't too freaked out by the clumsier-than-humanly-possible person walking toward them. An unfamiliar family stood waiting next to the player piano. Not that too many residents of the town looked familiar, but these people looked like they felt out of place. With their wide-eyed stares and the way the woman clung to the man's hand, something was unsettling them.

This wasn't a group happily going antique shopping. These people were afraid.

The dad stood in the back of the cluster, his eyes roaming the store, and one hand perched protectively on his daughter's shoulder. The mom held a toddler on her hip. The little boy looked like he'd found a candy store. I could only hope that she kept a tight grip on him, because if he got turned loose, hours of work in the front room would quickly turn into weeks' worth.

The girl was the one who stood out. The way she was staring at me while not looking at me made the hair on the back of my neck stand on end.

She was so thin that it looked like a strong gust of wind would knock her off her feet and so pale that I could easily see the web of veins running beneath the surface. Her skin hadn't seen the sunlight in weeks...or maybe years. She was definitely the most fragile-looking child I'd ever seen. But that wasn't her most outstanding feature.

True fear lived in the depths of those cocoa-tinted eyes.

Nails-on-a-chalkboard goosebumps raised on my skin. I'd seen something like this before. Just once. I didn't want to live through it again. I'd been too late to help that boy. A sick feeling washed over me, and if I believed in a god, I'd have been praying to him to make these people leave.

The parents turned to me with a desperation that I instantly understood. This girl didn't just look haunted. She *was* haunted.

"We're looking for Kate." The woman finally worked up the courage to speak, and she said exactly what I didn't want to hear.

Damn it. Kate *had* still been in the business. And this family knew it.

The mother swallowed, her lips forming a tight line. She was probably in her late twenties, but the fatigue and worry on her face made her look closer to fifty. Her teeth gnawed her lower lip. She was fighting with herself. Clearly confused at my presence, she turned back toward her husband, and he nodded her forward.

"Sorry. We're closed."

"We know. And we're sorry." The mother looked down at her free arm, checking the time on her watch. "But we're supposed to be here." Her voice sounded as tired as her face looked. As she spoke, her lower lip trembled. "But as I said, we had an appointment to see Kate. If you'll just find her, she's expecting us. She can explain."

"I'm sorry." I worked to sound honestly apologetic. "She's not here."

I wasn't sure why I didn't just say that Kate was dead— it wasn't that she didn't want to meet them; she couldn't meet them, even if she wanted to. And looking at the little girl, I know Kate would have wanted to.

"Can you call her? Maybe she just forgot. But we had an appointment." The father spoke with the gravity of a man whose daughter was going insane. If only it were that easy.

I'd never seen one so far gone. I wasn't sure if she was even seeing the real world any longer.

A spirit had her.

And not a kindly, Halloween-decoration kind of ghost. Someone wasn't ready to leave this world, so they'd latched onto her. She couldn't even be five yet.

"When was the last time you spoke to Kate?" I found my voice. Somehow, asking when they'd spoken last seemed easier than just blurting out the truth.

"I don't recall. But she was very specific. We had to come here today. This morning. The shop would be closed, but we were supposed to come in anyway. She told us where to find the spare key." The wife looked skittishly at her

146

husband with eyes that burned too bright. My avoiding calling Kate had alerted her to something.

I wanted to run. First, Kate told Mrs. Carter to expect me. Now, these people were here. Only one member of the family was strong enough to deal with a haunting like this.

Me.

How did Kate know I'd be here? She must have known something; she must have known she was going to die. That's the only way she'd be certain I would be here now. The room closed in around me, and I struggled to breathe. The pounding in my head felt like something was trying to split it in half.

"Is there a better time to meet with her?" The man kept throwing furtive looks out the window, as if he were scared of something.

That was it.

He was scared. They all were.

But why? Did they not want people to see they were here? Or was it something darker? Did they not want some*thing* to know they were here?

All the half-whispers and snippets of conversations I'd heard between my parents fell into place. My aunt had been practicing. My parents might have earned their living telling people ghost stories, but no one really believed they were real—even if they were.

Ghost stories were very real. I could attest to that.

But my aunt had told our secret. *My* secret.

Having these people here proved that much. But what could she do? She didn't have the gift. Or at least that's what my mom always said.

147

"Perhaps you can call her. Let her know the Ryder family is here." The dad was like a dog with a bone. He wasn't giving up without a fight.

"No. I'm sorry..." I cleared my throat, suddenly finding myself at a loss for words. My mom would get a laugh out of that. "Kate's not going to be able to help you."

"But she promised."

"We came all this way."

Their desperation threatened to send me into a panic. I could hardly stand to meet their eyes. And I couldn't look at the little girl, not knowing what I was about to tell them. "I'm Reese Everett. Kate passed away last week."

Their faces hung in the moment between shocked and despairing.

"We've tried everything. Everyone. Kate was our last hope."

The little girl looked back and forth between her parents, not following the conversation, but clearly able to sense their distress.

"What's wrong?" She glanced at me. "Where's the lady?"

"I'm sorry, sweetheart." I knelt on one knee, thankful for all my years of babysitting. "She's not here anymore. She passed away earlier this month."

The family seemed flustered. Caught off-guard by the news, the father took his daughter's hand.

"I guess we'll be going, then." Once again, the father spoke for the family. "I'm sorry to have bothered you."

The mother found her voice. "We're so sorry for your loss."

"Thanks." I shrugged it off. I didn't really do grief. "I appreciate it."

Before I could really think of anything else to say, they hurried from the shop. I was thankful they chose not to linger. I couldn't tell them what they wanted to hear.

Because I couldn't see the ghost.

I hadn't seen a ghost since I came into town, even when I wanted to. Even when I tried. Even when I knew one was hovering just inches from me. I saw...nothing.

But this little girl needed me. She needed what I could do—what I'd done in the past. I had to save her, even though I hadn't been able to save the other one. Nightmares were only supposed to live in dreams. That little girl had them when she was awake.

I couldn't get the expression in her eyes out of my head. I couldn't just let them go. Damn it, I was going to regret this. I chased after them, catching them while they were still on the porch.

"Wait. Just...wait." I beckoned them to follow me back into the shop. "Maybe I can help you."

The mother shook her head in a definite no, but the little girl moved toward me as if the decision was out of her control.

"Come here," I knelt down and waited for the girl to approach me. "What's your name?"

She glanced back at her mom for permission, and the woman nodded in agreement. I was thankful for that, since this worked better when I had a willing participant.

"Your name," I prompted.

"Quinn. Quinn Ryder."

"Hello, Quinn." I patted the floor in front of me as I knelt cross-legged on the floor. "Why don't you sit down?"

Most people think it takes candles, darkness, or weird chants to make the connection with the not-exactly-dead. That's not true. It simply takes someone strong enough...someone with a special sort of talent. A talent I typically possessed in abundance but that had failed me since I'd arrived in town.

Since I arrived in town.

The missing piece to the puzzle clicked itself into place. Now I understood why Mom had that last minute emergency errand to Davina that only I could complete. My mom's best witchy friend must have done something.

It was in the tea.

Her smile flashed in my memory as she pressed the cup into my hand. She'd insisted. Where were my manners? After she'd gone to all the trouble to make it. The least I could do would be to drink it.

When I got back to New Orleans, I was going to kill someone—if trying to find the ghosts here didn't kill me first. Because the ghosts were here. If I guessed right, they'd been all around me since I'd arrived.

I just couldn't see them because of whatever Davina had done.

Stretching out my hand, I took hold of the little girl's. Her fingers were as cold as death. She didn't have much time left. If I didn't help, I'd hear about her on the news some night—soon. Some kind of tragic accident most likely. Sometimes the dead are lonely.

"Your friend, is it a girl or a boy?" Quinn looked like she was going to die of shock. "It's all right. I know about your friend."

"How can you know about Ella?"

"Ella?" She knew the ghost's name. Never a good sign. This one was strong. Too strong for her. I hoped not too strong for me. "When did you meet her?"

She turned and stared back at her parents again. Clearly she'd been well-trained in the topic of not talking about Ella, a friend that even her parents couldn't see but who was all too real. And definitely not a friend.

"You can tell her, Quinn."

"She just showed up one day."

"Had you recently brought anything new into the house?" This time, my question was for the parents, one of whom was trying to pretend this conversation wasn't happening while the other held onto my every word like I was saving her from drowning. "I mean, anything old. Something at a garage sale? Maybe a family heirloom?"

The dad nodded. "We'd found an old rocking horse at an antique store."

"You put it in her room?"

"No." The mother's voice was choked and indistinct. "It was in Brogan's."

She was holding the little boy's hand in a vice-tight grip. He appeared to want to do anything other than stand here now, watching me talk with his sister. God, I hoped I was only dealing with one haunting here. I leaned to the side, trying to catch his eye.

I'd never been good with kids. They just didn't like me. Sometimes I thought they knew I could see more than just the world everyone else could see. Or at least I normally could. Not right now.

But right now I had to try.

151

"Brogan, would you like some candy? I have some chocolate bars next to the cash register." That did the trick. His green eyes met mine. Thankfully, I only saw the bright-eyed interest prompted by the mention of chocolate.

So the furniture was in his room, but the ghost latched onto his sister. Different, but not the first time I'd heard of it. She was probably closer to Quinn's age than his. Quinn would appear to be a good playmate.

A living playmate.

My headache was worse now, stronger, like a giant was squeezing my head between its fingertips. Much more pressure, and it would explode. Davina must have built this into her spell, assuming I'd give up when the pain hit.

The witch didn't know me as well as she thought she did.

Metal clattered in the storage room. I must have left the vintage coffee pots off-balance by the sound of it. I couldn't think about that now. Not when I had a far more pressing matter at hand.

I closed my eyes, fighting past whatever she'd done to mask my ability. The harder I pushed, the sharper the pain. Even with my eyes shut, pinpricks of light appeared in my field of vision. I fought to focus like I'd never tried before. I was not going to fail this little one. Tears swam down my cheeks, and I was fighting a losing battle with the contents of my stomach.

"Are you quite all right?" A new young voice sounded in the room.

I opened my eyes without hesitation. Ella was standing off to the side of Quinn. Despite asking the question, she appeared disinterested in me, all her attention focused on the coloring book. I could only imagine what the coloring book turning its own pages must look like to the others in the room. Right now, I couldn't check to see. Right now, I had to use all my strength on keeping her here.

"Ella?"

She glanced at me, her attention confirming her name. Her colorless eyes seemed sad. "This one isn't finished."

"Do you like to color?" I'd noticed an oversized pile of them in the corner of the room. Kate must have kept them for the younger clients.

"I like to draw." Her freckles stood out against the paleness of her cheeks. For someone with almost jet-black hair, her skin was an unexpected shade of white. Ella almost looked like any other little girl—except for the whole kind-of-transparent thing.

Judging from her clothing, I'd say she was probably alive back at the turn of the century. The little girl's braids rested softly on her shoulders while she slowly paged through an old coloring book. The fact that she could turn pages so effortlessly wasn't a good sign.

If I'd been any other seer, I might have run in fear.

Quinn was lucky I was here and not Kate. I pushed harder. Now that I knew what the problem was, I could shove the pain to the side, at least for the moment. Ella seemed to sense it...sense I was coming for her. She blinked in surprise, taking a half-step back from the table.

"Are you Quinn's friend?"

"I try to be." The coldness in her eyes showed she was anything other than a friend.

"She doesn't want you to stay with her. It's time for you to go."

"But I like her." An angry flush crawled up her neck. Crap. An angry ghost in the middle of an antique store.

"You need to leave her alone."

"I don't want to." Fire shone in Ella's eyes. Her voice was peppered with the energy she possessed, energy she'd claimed from Quinn. "She doesn't want me to leave either."

One patent leather shoe in front of the other, she strode confidently across the floor before taking Quinn's hand.

I didn't think Quinn could have gotten any paler. I was wrong.

"I told you to leave." I stood, claiming the strength I'd refined from years of experience in the darkened streets of home. My left hand clutched my right wrist, and I felt the tiny beads pressing into my flesh.

"No."

"Go!" I commanded with so much energy it hurt. For a second, everything around me blurred. My ears filled with the hollow sound of seashells on the beach. A rush of power I'd never had at my command before rushed through me.

Everything in the room seemed to move in stop motion. I caught glimpses of the world around me, but it was like a slide show played out before my eyes.

Ella was there. Then she wasn't.

Then she was just in front of me.

Then she wasn't a sweet little girl anymore. Her face contorted into something that would fill my broken dreams at night.

But then she was gone.

When my vision returned, Quinn had scampered back to stand with her parents. "Where'd she go?" Her voice was a mixture of confusion and relief.

"Somewhere she won't bother you again."

"She's gone?" Mr. Ryder found his ability to speak first.

"She's gone," I agreed.

"Will she come back?" Mrs. Ryder had picked Brogan up and shielded him from me like I was the dangerous one in the room.

"No."

"You're sure?" She wasn't convinced.

"I'm certain. Quinn's friend is gone."

Mr. Ryder reached into his back pocket, and I was confused for a moment. Then I realized he was getting his wallet. He wanted to pay me. "How much?"

"No charge." I waved him off. The sound of a door shutting came from behind me, and I was confused since there wasn't an exit back there.

"But when we spoke with Kate..."

I shook my head, my headache was back with me, buzzing around like a pesky fly. The energy in the building had changed. I was the one who'd changed it. I'd ripped a hole in the psychic veil Davina had wrapped around me.

"Is there anything else?" The Ryders were still standing there, staring at me. I must have fit the description of a crazy lady who could see ghosts by now.

"No. You're fine. Just be careful with the antiques from now on." I fought back a laugh, since I was standing in the middle of an antique shop. I suspected nothing here was sold until it passed Kate's inspection.

"Thank you." I wasn't even sure which one of them said it.

"You're welcome."

And they hurried through the front door in a manner that suggested I frightened them as much as Ella had. Maybe more. I dropped back down to the ground, covering my eyes with my hand, struggling not to be sick.

Time passed.

Seconds, minutes, hours—I wasn't sure. I wasn't sure of anything until I heard footsteps on the porch.

"Reese?" The bell to the front door tinkled as Shelby's voice sailed into the store. "Are you here? I saw those people leaving, and I wanted to pop in to check to see if everything was all right. I guess they were angry when they found out you were closed. Kate always got a slew of visitors during Heritage Days. Are you here?"

"Back here. On the floor." I opened my eyes a crack, just in time to see the overly-friendly owner of the shop next door trotted up beside me. Based on her overly wide eyes, I must have looked worse than I felt. I closed my eyes again. The whole looking-around thing wasn't working so well with the whole trying-not-to-vomit thing.

"Are you all right?"

"Migraine. I get them sometimes."

"Do you need anything?" She leaned down, placing a hand on my shoulder. Her worried-meter had gone past ten and hit eleven.

"No. It'll pass." I stayed on the ground, suspecting that I wasn't going to be successful at standing upright at this moment.

"You're sure?"

"Yeah." *Breathe in through the nose. Out through the mouth.* Or was it the other way around? I couldn't remember, but it appeared to be helping. "See? It's all good."

I stood, still shaky, now that the flood of adrenaline was leaching away.

"I'll trust you." She cocked her head to the side, still examining me with suspicion.

"Did you need something else?"

Shelby bit her lip, appearing to be trying to decide if she wanted to bother me or not. "This probably isn't the best time."

"No, go ahead. I could use a distraction."

"It's about the shop. I was talking with some of the other store owners." The corners of her eyes wrinkled, and her forehead furrowed. If she drew her nose up, she'd be doing an impression of a rabbit. Her words had taken on such a sweet tone, I was surprised they weren't dripping honey. "Have y'all decided what you're doing with it?"

"I think my mom wants to sell it." I didn't think; I knew. I'd gotten no fewer than five voicemails telling me to hurry up so they could sell and I could get back home.

"I was afraid of that." Her shoulders slumped. She took a moment to regain composure before turning her eyes back on me. "Sad to hear you're giving this place up. It's so important these days to carry on the family business."

No. I massaged my temples with one hand while closing my eyes, hoping she would think the migraine still had me in its grip. Tradition or not, I had no desire to be in the family business—at least not the one that Shelby knew nothing about.

Now that I'd broken through whatever spell Davina had cast on me, a sense of dread filled my chest at the thought of returning home. Spirits seldom frightened me. But it felt as if something had changed since I'd returned to Devil's Vale.

Chapter Thirteen

Colton

Dad was going to be thrilled. At least he'd better be. I still couldn't believe the message on my voicemail. Everything was set. The school board had given their approval. Georgia's Department of Education had granted a temporary waiver for my lack of teaching certification because of the special circumstances surrounding the job.

Special circumstances.

Why didn't anyone come out and say it? No one wanted the job since the last coach shot himself in the head while standing in the middle of his office. That didn't exactly make people line up to replace him.

Now I had to find Dad to tell him the news. If I hurried, maybe I wouldn't have to watch him gloat. Without stopping at the cabin, I drove up to the main house. His car was in the driveway. That was a good sign. Part of me wondered if I even needed to tell him the news. Since Rick had been so good about keeping him in the information loop, my dad probably knew the school board's decision before I did.

After I parked in the same spot I'd used since my granddad had given the truck to me, I hopped down from the driver's seat and tucked the keys into my pocket, not bothering to lock it. My mom hadn't been exaggerating when she hinted it was on borrowed time. Even eighty thousand miles was a distant memory to that truck.

I walked up the marble patio stairs, becoming more aware of a general sense of dread with each step. I didn't knock on the front door. After all my dad's lectures about the responsibility I had to the family, I shouldn't have to wait for one of the housekeepers to let me in. So I let myself in, surprised at how happy the little act of rebellion made me.

I stood at the bottom of the main stairs, listening. My father's office was empty, and the den was dark too. He was here somewhere, but I wasn't about to just start yelling in the house. Voices drifted down the stairs. Someone must be up there—that was as good a place as any to start looking, so I jogged up the staircase.

"I'm telling you, I know what I saw."

Shelby's voice was talking-on-a-speakerphone loud. Even through her closed bedroom door, I could tell she was pacing. What the hell was she doing home at this time of day? She'd convinced Mom to turn the candle shop over to her last year. If I'd heard one lecture about the responsibilities of being a business owner, I'd heard twenty. And she was in her room talking on the phone?

"Listen."

"I am listening." The voice that answered wasn't our dad, but it was way too familiar. "I'm just telling you that you didn't see what you thought you saw. Hell, you didn't really see anything. Didn't you say you were in the storage room?"

My sister was talking to Max?

Max.

The same guy I'd hung out with every day since we were in diapers. The guy who stood next to me at my first football game. The one who held me on his shoulder when we won state. My friend who hadn't called me in weeks.

"I needed to be sure." Shelby didn't sound like she was talking to a casual friend.

"So you went in through the back door. Way to not seem suspicious."

"I was trying to help."

I knew I should have walked away. No way did Shelby realize I could hear every word, and I was sure Max didn't know they had an audience for the discussion.

"And then I came in through the front door." The familiar spray of an aerosol can told me Shelby was stress cleaning. Never a good sign. "She was wearing the bracelet."

"How in hell did she get that?" A hint of uncertainty darkened Max's voice. He sounded like he did in the locker room our junior year when we were down by fourteen points at halftime.

"If I knew, do you think I'd be talking to you right now?"

"No one's seen that bracelet in—"

"A hundred years," Shelby interrupted. If he'd been in the room right now, he'd need to be worried.

"Listen, I know you're nervous since Kate…"

"Since Kate what?" My sister interrupted him with an intensity that should have frightened him if he'd been in the same room with her.

"You know."

"What I know is you need to get back here."

"You've got it covered."

"That's the problem. I don't think I do. You didn't see her. Max, I can't do this alone. I was never supposed to. It's starting."

Just when I was ready to storm through the door to confront both of them, heavy footfalls sounded on the stairs. Boots thudded up the stairs one by one. I'd come up here to find my dad and found something far more interesting. But now he'd found me.

"Colton." Dad was puffing as he mounted the last step. "Just got a message from Rick." He waved his phone in the air. "He said you have good news for me."

"Yeah." I could still hear Shelby, but now her voice was just a whisper. She must have heard Dad in the hallway. "Good news."

"Well, come on down. We'll have a drink to celebrate." He started to go down the stairs without watching to see if I followed. He knew I would. In twenty-three years, I'd only stood up to him once. I'd never been brave enough since.

But I didn't want a drink.

I wanted to get in my truck, ride out of town, and never come back. I couldn't, though. Because the only back stockroom Shelby knew how to sneak into was at Daze Gone By.

Something was up. I'd known it since Coach died. Before then, really.

I'd seen it in the way Dad looked at me. I'd noticed it in the way Shelby didn't always answer my questions. And I was sure things were off when Max had disappeared. It was time I started getting some answers.

"You coming?"

But first I was having an un-celebratory drink with my father.

ß

I'd barely been able to escape my father's new-job celebration. If I hadn't reminded him that his best friend Rick was waiting for me to clean up, put on a polo and khakis, and be back at the school by five, I wouldn't have been able to get away. But one mention of Rick's name, and I'd been shooed out the front door like a fly with a warning not to be late to the parents' meeting.

Who called a parents' meeting just hours after deciding to hire someone anyway? I doubted the ink was dry yet on my contract. But here I was, just minutes from being announced as the new coach. He must have wanted to beat the town gossips to the punch.

If I seemed even the slightest bit doubtful about taking the job, the people in that auditorium would destroy me. I'd seen the roster. I'd been on a team with a half-dozen of the guys' older brothers. The people out there knew me a little too well. So I knew the drill. Fake it until you make it.

I waited in the wings of the stage at the high school auditorium. I resented this job in the first place, and I hated it even more knowing it was keeping me from seeing Reese tonight. I hadn't seen her since Sunday. Three days. She probably thought I'd given up on the house. I'd be lucky if she hadn't called Bud to replace me.

I didn't want to be replaced.

What was wrong with me? I didn't get bent of out shape because I couldn't see a girl. All I had to do was pick up my phone and answer one of the half-dozen text messages I'd gotten since I was back in town. I was Colton Waters. Girls chased me.

"You ready?" A coach who'd started working at the school after my graduation came up and rested a hand on my shoulder like he'd known me for years. I brushed it off.

Only one coach knew me close enough to get that close...and he was dead. That's why I was here.

My stomach knotted, realizing everyone out in that room felt the same way about me as I did this new guy. They were suspicious I couldn't carry on where Coach had left off. They were right.

While I was certain they were wondering who'd carry on after Max's dad was gone, I couldn't help feeling that if the rest of the coaches kept looking, they'd find someone else better suited for the job.

I'd just been introduced to rest of the coaches this afternoon after the paperwork was officially signed, even though most of the introductions weren't really necessary. I hadn't been out of school that long. Each one of my now-coworkers had been a coach of mine at some point while I was back in school. Being announced to the kids who'd be playing for Devil's Vale next year just felt oddly permanent.

"You ready for this?" Coach Price slapped an arm on my shoulder. He'd been the one who seemed least surprised to see me. He even offered to meet for coffee some morning to go over our strategy for next season.

"I'm not quite sure."

"Then you're definitely ready." Coach Smith approached with a nod. "The second you think you have things under control is generally when all hell breaks loose."

I couldn't have summed it up better.

Rick—he insisted that I call him Rick now—sped past on his way to the podium. I'd never seen things from this side of the stage before. I'd spent plenty of time in the seats that needed renovating, but I'd never stared out at the sea of faces.

How would they react?

"Hello!" Rick's voice boomed into the room, and feedback buzzed back to greet him. "I guess the sound system's still on summer break."

He chuckled at his own joke, and the assembled audience laughed along with him. It would be funnier if it weren't so true.

Rick tried again, with more success this time. He waved out to the crowd like a contestant at a beauty pageant acknowledging the judges. "Good to see so many of y'all could join us. I know it's a little unexpected for me to invite you all here during summer break, but based on the e-mails and voicemails I've been getting, everyone's eager to hear who'll be joining our coaching staff."

I was relieved it didn't sound like he was going to spend too much time dwelling on what happened to Max's dad. One memorial service was enough. Sometimes everyone just needed to move on.

"I'm pretty sure a few of you have heard the news already." Based on the mumbling in the crowd, that was a yes. "So I'll get right to it. First up, we'll be promoting John Price to head coach."

My favorite history teacher stepped past me amid fairly hearty applause. Coach Price was everyone's favorite if I had to be honest. I'd never met a kid who didn't like him, and I'd never heard him chew out a player on the field. I wasn't sure just how effective he'd be as head coach, but I couldn't complain about working for him. Rick shook his hand and clapped his shoulder before nodding to signal he was turning the rest of the meeting over to Coach Price. He took the stairs two at a time as if he couldn't wait to get off the stage.

Coach Price started talking, and I should have been listening.

I should have been listening to hear what he thought about the team, the coaching staff, and our chances for next season.

But I wasn't.

Because at that exact moment, I saw movement at the back door of the auditorium. If I'd been standing two feet closer to the curtain, I would have missed it. As it was, I had to do a double-take.

My dad had just walked into the meeting.

Being proud of your hometown football team or supporting your kid in their new job is one thing. But walking up to your son's new boss and giving him a man-hug, complete with a thump on the middle of the back was totally something else.

I knew Dad and Rick were friends. Heck, they used to go fishing once a year, and Rick was part of the guys-who-drink-coffee-and-pretend-they're-not-gossiping thing most Saturday mornings down at Mugs.

Right now, they looked like best friends.

One best friend who'd just given the other's son a job.

I couldn't put my finger on it, but this whole thing had felt off. They chatted away like old ladies at the hair salon in the back corner of the auditorium while they should have been listening to Coach Price talk.

That was why my dad was here, wasn't it? To be part of the kickoff for the season, to watch as his son was announced as a new coach. So why did it feel more like they didn't really care about what was going on at the meeting, not as long as their plan for me to work at the high school was working?

"Coach Waters?" Coach Price was stifling a laugh, waving for me to take my place at his side. I was the only member of the staff not currently in the middle of the stage. He gripped my shoulders with a strength that showed he was once an award-winning wide receiver. "Gonna take a little while to get used to that new title, isn't it?"

"Yes, sir. Yes it is." I tried to play along with his lighthearted joke. He was trying to cover for the fact that I hadn't been listening, and I appreciated it since not all the parents looked like they were convinced I should be part of the staff.

Looking out, I saw more than a few familiar faces—the younger siblings of guys on one of my teams and some parents who used to buy us pizza when we hung out at their houses after a game. But as I scanned the back of the crowd, I only saw a sliver of light through the rapidly closing door.

Rick stood alone now, arms crossed. I wouldn't have known that just seconds ago, he'd been talking excitedly with my father.

Because now, just as I stepped to the podium, I could see that my dad was gone. Of course he was. What else was new? He wasn't there for me—not to watch his son make his first official coach pep-talk. He'd came to see Rick, probably to thank him for hiring me...doing my dad a favor.

But had Rick done the favor? Or was it my dad?

As I stared out at the sea of faces staring at me, many of them wearing expressions that signaled more than just a hint of suspicion, I remembered a day that I was just as confused as they seemed to be now. I hadn't understood why I'd been suddenly un-accepted to medical school.

What if Rick wasn't the one doing the favor? What if that honor went to my dad? But that would mean...

I'd found out about medical school before Max's dad shot himself. My dad couldn't have seen that one coming. Still, I couldn't help the nagging sense of dread. Things had fallen into place too easily. Nothing in Devil's Vale was ever this simple.

Chapter Fourteen
❧☙

Reese

I'd tossed and turned all night. No matter what my mom said, Kate had been practicing.

I wanted...no, I *needed* to figure out where.

And the fact that the family had appeared at the shop during business hours instead of at her house in the dead of night told me one thing—she'd been keeping up the family business at the antique shop. Besides, the house might be cluttered, but I'd already examined it thoroughly enough to know that there wasn't a hidden room somewhere back there.

It was at the shop. It had to be.

And knowing Kate's flair for the dramatic, I'd know it when I found it.

My car rolled to a stop in front of the store just in time to see Shelby stepping out of her Prius in the shady corner of the candle shop. She paused on the front steps, looking up from her phone, and gave a hint of a wave. For a second it looked like she was going to say something, but a chirp of her phone distracted her, and she looked down with a frown.

I didn't have time to waste with idle chatter anyway. I had work to do. I stepped out of my truck, taking the time to really look at the building. It wasn't too remarkable, just a

169

little wooden framed house. A covered patio protected the entire front porch. I followed the roof line around the corner and counted five windows. That matched up with what I remembered from inside the main room of the shop. I crossed in front of the house, circling around to the other side. Three plain windows then a section of bay windows in what was once the dining room.

And then in the back...one more. A tiny window, not more than a foot by two feet, stood high above my head, way too far above me to peek in. Too high for me to even really notice. That's why I hadn't seen it before.

That and the fact that I hadn't found the room yet.

I'd already explored the whole house. Or at least I thought I had. Clearly I was wrong.

My pulse raced like when I stood in line for my favorite roller coaster.

The shop had a secret room.

A fuzzy memory tried to emerge. I'd loved playing detective when I was little. A girl with cornstalk-yellow hair skulked through an unfamiliar house with me. A boy paused in front of us, turning around...shushing our laughter as we tried to solve whatever made up mystery we'd concocted.

Who were they? I brushed the question aside.

Right now, finding Kate's room took priority. I only had time for one unsolved mystery at the moment. I unlocked the door, walked through the main display area, and opened the door to step into the tiny store room that must have been a bedroom. Nothing here.

I crossed the kitchen and the former dining room, now used to display a collection of rare books. To my right was the large storeroom. I'd already spent hours in there. It spanned the length of the house, didn't it? Much like Kate's house, boxes and random items were stacked almost to the ceiling, but I could still make out all four walls.

No windows.

I backed out of the room and turned to face the book area. Most of the wall was dominated by a shelving structure. I walked next to the wall and knocked.

It echoed.

Only mildly surprised at this point, I backed away. I examined all the wallpaper—not a single hole, rip, or change in pattern. There wasn't a door along the wall. As I'd been reminded by the fire marshal, there wasn't a door in the back of the house either.

But something was back there.

Kate would have wanted it to be easy to enter but not too easy. No one could randomly happen upon her room, so she would have been careful to keep secreted away. I walked to the bookshelf and began to examine the books. I pressed them and pulled them, tugged them and tipped them on their sides.

Nothing.

Each of the books felt like a book. None of them revealed any type of secret passage. Maybe my mind was playing tricks on me. The window must just be hidden behind one of the piles of boxes, and I didn't see it.

"All right, Kate, show me your secrets." I spoke into thin air, moderately annoyed that I'd spent so much time on this wild goose chase. I stood, planning to walk back into the storage room. My arm brushed against a stack as I got to my feet, and a well-worn copy of *Macbeth* tumbled to the ground.

A little too worn to be honest. Kate was particular about her books. Bring in one with mold or silverfish, and she could kiss her whole collection goodbye. I picked it up. It was far too light.

No way. My heart skipped a beat as I cracked it open.

It wasn't a book. At least it wasn't a book anymore. Someone had wanted it to look like a book, but the pages were pasted together with a hollow cut out at the center. A tiny remote control sat hidden in the center of the book.

Had secret rooms gone high tech?

I pressed the button, and something clicked behind the bookshelf. I guessed the answer to my question was yes.

Not sure what to expect, I swung the bookshelf open. Whatever I'd thought, it wasn't what was staring back at me.

When I was little and Aunt Kate had come to visit, she'd loved to tell me stories about places she'd visited and people she'd met—back before it was her turn to mind the store. I'd always thought some of her stories were exaggerations. No one could have done that many things. No one lived that kind of life.

I stepped down into her hidden room, and I wondered if I'd known Kate at all. Somehow I doubted it.

I'd thought this room was small, but I'd far underestimated it. It really wasn't much smaller than the library I'd just left. The walls were covered with deep crimson wallpaper, the kind you'd find in a house at the turn of the century. The turn of the twentieth century, of course. Apart from a little dust, the room was spotless. It didn't take a psychic to know what she'd used this room for—lamps with lace, pictures of women in high-necked dresses, high-backed chairs covered in velvet, mahogany occasional tables.

And a Ouija board that clearly didn't come from a toy store.

It was a parlor from ages ago. Someone from the Civil War era would have been comfortable walking in. The bookshelves were covered with thick, leather-bound tomes, books written lifetimes ago. I craned my neck to read the titles. Not all of them were in English.

A Pictorial Reference of the Civil War

Enchantements de Protection

Modern Day History of the Occult

Battle Sites in Georgia

A shiver ran up my spine. My mother always said no one else in the family could do what I could. My mother was wrong.

This room was Kate's stage. Judging from the age of the furniture and the heavy scent of sage and wood smoke hanging in the air, it had belonged to someone long before her.

I took my time walking around, studying, not even certain what I was looking for. I just knew I needed to find...it. But I didn't even know what *it* was. Still, I was certain this room held all the answers.

How had Kate know I'd be coming?

I finally approached the circular table in the middle of the room under the black, beaded chandelier. I'd never seen one like it.

Dark light for dark arts.

A chair's arms worn smooth from use, wooden box in middle of table, and ledger written in Kate's handwriting answered one question. Lots of people had come here for her services. And another—how she had stayed in business. With the amount of visitors she'd had, she could have likely kept half the shops in town in business.

There were letters—mainly people thanking Kate for helping them find peace— newspaper clippings, a recipe for lemon sponge pie, and a letter...for me.

> My Dear Reese –
> If you're here and you've found this, I'm saddened to say all the visions I've had of late have come to pass. And I'm sorry. I apologize for not being able to tell you...to explain to you in person.
> I was never in favor of keeping the secret from you. The secret of who I am. The secret of who you are.
> Dangerous times are coming. You need to be prepared. If you're here, then it's already on its way.
> Trust yourself.
> And remember that few here are exactly what they seem.
> All my love,
> Kate

I rocked back on my heels, allowing the yellowed paper to float to the floor. I glared at the letter. *Few people here are what they seem.* Well, that was just wonderful.

A few specifics would have been nice, maybe a list of who exactly I could trust.

"Come on, Kate." I leaned back, allowing my hands to catch my weight, while I stared at the haint-blue ceiling and tried not to laugh at the irony. "Can you just give me one hint of who I can trust?

The front door jingled open, almost giving me a heart attack.

I shot to my feet, determined to get the secret door shut before anyone caught a glimpse of this room. Heading to the foyer, I had a lecture about privacy and waiting for someone to answer the door on the tip of my tongue before I saw who'd arrived.

If Colton standing in front of me right now was a sign from beyond, Kate knew how to pick them.

"Do you have a thing about not answering your door? You almost let the burgers get cold." Colton held up a brown paper sack. The smell of something greasy and fried drifted in my direction.

"It can't be lunchtime." I'd just gotten to the store a few minutes ago, maybe an hour.

"It's almost twelve." He held out his arm, displaying his watch.

My stomach didn't growl as much as it roared to life, happily reminding me that it truly was lunchtime. He gave the bag a shake. The rustle sounded suspiciously like fries.

"I ran by Al's. It was time for you to try the green chile cheeseburger."

"Sure."

Colton started walking in the direction of the kitchen area. "Hope you don't mind. I didn't want you to eat alone. And I wanted to celebrate."

"Celebrate? What are we celebrating?"

He paused and looked back at me. A glimmer came into his eyes, and he raised an eyebrow. "I'm officially employed."

"Congratulations."

"Don't sound so excited."

"Sorry." I didn't want to put an additional damper on the mood, but he seemed less than thrilled as well. "I am happy for you."

Then the weight of his news hit me, and I forgot to breathe. If he was working somewhere, then who'd do the last repairs on the house?

"Don't worry. I don't officially start for a few more weeks. I haven't forgotten about retiling that upstairs shower. I won't let you down any more than I have already. Sorry I've been scarce. This week has been...odd."

"Tell me about it," I mumbled, but he was too busy riffling through the bag to hear me. The heavenly scent of fried potatoes filled the air between us as he dumped an extra-large order onto a pile of napkins.

"Do you have drinks in here? I forgot to grab any." He wandered across the break room to the tiny refrigerator and leaned over with his head in the fridge, giving me an excellent view of exactly how well his jeans fit. He could take his time.

"Yeah. Look in the bottom drawer."

"You keep cans in the drawer?"

"Trick from college." I pulled the chair out and sat at the table opposite his seat. "Most people stay out of the vegetable drawer. You didn't look there, did you?"

"Smart." He looked impressed. "What other tricks are you hiding up your sleeve?"

I shook my head and averted my eyes. "Not many."

Just one gigantic one. One so large, he'd drop me the instant he found out. I'd been there, done that. The outcome wasn't pretty.

Colton held up two drinks, asking which I wanted without saying a word. I pointed to the diet soda, and he tossed it to me. "Come on. You've spent your life digging through the leftover tidbits of other people's lives. You have to know a few dark secrets."

Oh, I knew a great many dark secrets. I just couldn't share them.

"It's not that interesting." I opened a packet of ketchup and poured it onto the corner of waxed paper the hamburger had been wrapped in. "Most of the time, it's just doing battle against the dust, mold, and spiders."

"Spiders." He repeated, his nose wrinkling.

"Not a fan of spiders?"

"Not exactly."

I couldn't keep from laughing.

"What's so funny about that?" He tossed a handful of fries into his mouth.

"Just the mental picture. You're a big, strong football coach."

"Who just happens to be freaked out by things with eight legs." He shivered, emphasizing his words.

"Remind me not to take you down into the basement."

He stopped chewing. "Basement?"

"Not here. Back at Kate's house. I found a door behind the boxes at the end of the hall. I haven't been brave enough to go down there yet, but I think there's a basement."

"You mean the root cellar. It's not very big. I doubt she'd manage getting too much stuff down those stairs." His eyebrows knit together with concern. "Be careful. Who knows how long it's been since anyone's gone down those stairs. They might be rotten."

"I'll be careful." Once again, Colton knew Kate's house far better than I did. Why did that bother me? I took a bite of the hamburger. The oozing cheese combined with the hint of spice from the peppers, reminded me just how long it had been since I'd eaten. I was going to have to stop forgetting meals.

He was staring at me.

Not just looking. *Staring* staring.

I'd thought I'd felt my cheeks flush before, but now they positively burned, and it had absolutely nothing to do with the peppers on the burger. He licked an invisible crumb from his lower lip, and my breath hitched. I swallowed— twice.

If he didn't make a move soon, I was going to clear the tiny table and do it myself. I was a strong, independent woman. I could do it.

Colton saved me the trouble. He reached across the table, initially making a move like he was going to pretend to wipe a smudge from my cheek before he just went for it. His fingertips pressed against my jaw first. Then his thumb skimmed my cheek, and my skin felt like it was going to ignite.

I wasn't sure who stood first, but we were on our feet, lunch completely forgotten.

His lips hovered millimeters from mine. His breath was hot on my cheek. I'd have been surprised if he couldn't feel my racing pulse beneath his fingertips. By the hint of a grin on his lips, he did.

Those lips.

I didn't want to see them smiling. I didn't want to see them at all. I wanted to feel them pressed against mine. I'd dreamed about those lips. I'd thought about them as I sorted candlesticks. I'd wondered if they'd be soft and needy or hard and in control.

His free hand brushed my side, finding a home at my waist. He pulled me in, and our lips connected. I had my answer. His kiss was soft and yet demanding. He gave a low groan that vibrated through his chest, and I knew he'd been wanting this...no, needing this as long as I had.

Everything in the room that wasn't us faded into distant memory.

Heat built low in my belly, and a familiar stir churned deep in my core. He pulled me closer against him, and I could feel every well-toned muscle pressed into my chest. A hint of wetness struck my mouth as his tongue slid against my lips.

The hand on my jaw moved back to my neck as his fingers tangled in my hair. He pulled my lips tighter against his than I'd thought possible. I was almost embarrassed as a sigh escaped my lips, but he seized the opportunity and plunged his tongue into the space, skimming against my teeth.

He pressed one leg between mine, and I almost came undone. When his hand on my waist traveled beneath the pockets of my jeans, cupping my rear, I felt the evidence of how much he was turned on pushing against me.

"Excuse me."

I almost bit the tip of Colton's tongue as I recoiled in shock. Mrs. Carter stood less than three feet away. She'd gotten quite a show. If she'd been five minutes later, I was fairly certain she would have gotten a lesson in human sexuality. Judging by the way she shifted back and forth between her sensible pumps, she could have used it.

Preserving any shred of dignity was a no-go, so I went on the attack. "What are you doing here?"

She gave a scolding clearing of her throat. "I came to check on the progress of the renovation plans."

I fought the urge to say that she could screw the floor plans, but I wasn't sure if using the word screw right now was the best idea. Colton hadn't said a word, but he'd shuffled behind me in visible discomfort.

That made two of us. My entire body was screaming that it wasn't quite finished yet. "I told you on Monday that I'd have the plans for you next week."

"The Ladies of the Society requested a progress report."

The ladies wanted a report. Did they meet for lunch or something? I ran a hand over my face, hoping it wiped some of the color off but knowing that was unlikely. "I've got some ideas. Nothing on paper yet."

"We were hoping to present the plans during Heritage Days."

Of course they needed it before Heritage Days was over. "That goes through next week, right?"

"Yes." If I'd thought she was cold during our earlier dealings, she'd moved into iceberg territory. "The festival ends on Friday."

"And I said I'd have the designs for you Monday. That's plenty of time."

"You seem...preoccupied." The shame she attached to the last word made it seem like we'd been stripped naked and doing it in the middle of the breakroom floor. "You can't lose sight of why you're here."

My muscles tensed, and I started to sweat. But it had nothing to do with what Colton and I had been doing just minutes before.

"What or *who* I'm doing doesn't concern you." If my mom knew I'd been kissing a guy, she'd have been celebrating, not giving me a glare suggesting she was measuring me for a scarlet letter. "I'll have the plans for you by Monday. If you leave me alone, I might even work faster."

I stared in the direction of the door. I almost didn't believe it when she took the hint.

"See that you do." It figured she'd be one of the ones who had to get the last word in during an argument. She left without a backward glance. I followed her to the door, sliding the latch to the deadlock into place.

But it was too late. Colton was clearing the last of the lunch mess off the table while shaking his head like he knew something I didn't. After he dropped the bags into the trash, he leaned against the counter, the right corner of his lips raised up in amusement. "*Who* you do?"

"She drives me crazy."

"She drives everyone crazy." His lips puckered, and I could see his lip tracing the outline of his teeth despite his closed mouth. "But you need to watch yourself around her. She's not someone you want as an enemy."

Chapter Fifteen
ॐ

The shop's electricity was turned off. I stared at the switch, toggling it up and down. I knew Kate had paid the bill. I saw the check number in her business ledger. Mrs. Carter had probably gotten it shut off so I had to focus on the house. She seemed like the type who could snap her fingers and folks in town would do whatever she asked.

Colton was right. That woman was dangerous.

Although being alone with him was just as dangerous. I had little doubt that if we hadn't been interrupted, we'd have tested the integrity of the bed set up in the mock-bedroom at the back of the shop. It seemed sturdy enough.

As it was, once Mrs. Carter left, Colton suddenly found his shoes interesting...and the activity out the window...and the crack running through the ceiling. He did everything in his power not to focus on me. When his phone rang and he excused himself, it was almost a relief.

Was I really ready for this?

I'd never felt anything like kissing Colton before, and I'd dated some pretty awesome kissers. When his lips had touched mine, I'd been surprised fireworks hadn't exploded over our heads.

When he'd left, I couldn't tell exactly how he'd felt. Had he thought the kiss was a mistake? He'd scurried out the

182

door like someone had lit a fire under his heels. I had the vague suspicion the kiss had been a one-time thing.

I really hoped not, since half my dreams last night revolved around places his hands hadn't quite explored yet. I was beyond screwed.

And now I was stuck in the dark.

Just my luck that the day I decided to go in to the shop early, I wouldn't have power. I glanced out a side window and noticed a light in the candle shop. Shelby struck me as more of a daddy's-money kind of girl than someone who actually worked hard at the business. Was she already at work?

There was only one way to find out. I stepped out the door and crossed the short distance between our stores. Her front door was cute in a Pinterest kind of way. The dove-gray door was the perfect shabby-chic accent to the pale pink building. A spray of dried flowers was tied with a tea-darkened linen ribbon. If I were planning on keeping Kate's shop open, I'd need to talk with Shelby about some decorating ideas. Right now, the front of the store was so tightly packed with Kate's treasures that I was surprised anyone bought anything.

I'd need some help bringing order to the chaos.

What was I thinking? I wasn't keeping Kate's store open. And I wasn't doing myself any good just standing on the porch admiring the neighbor's décor. I could examine the decorations on my last day in town.

I hesitated in front of the door for a second. Since her lights were on, that kind of answered my question, although it didn't solve my working-in-the-dark issue. I almost turned and walked away, but the door swung open before I laid a hand on it. I took a tentative step inside, unsure who'd opened it for me.

Yes, Reese, go right inside the apparently empty building. Don't worry about the door opening by itself. I wouldn't survive living in a horror movie. "Hello?"

"Hey, Reese. I saw you coming. Just give me a second. I'm at a critical stage back here. Just look around." Shelby's somewhat muffled voice came from the back of the shop, accompanied by clanks and a swishing sound I assumed was probably a spoon in a pot.

"Thanks. I'll just look around."

Way to go, Reese. Now you're seeing creepy where creepy doesn't exist.

Shelby had seen me walking over. That explained the door opening—nothing supernatural about it. I started in the candle section, pleased to notice an absence of sugary-sweet candles trying to imitate confections. Instead, she seemed to prefer natural scents.

I selected a candle that reminded me of the color of the sunset over the gulf. Lifting the glass lid, I took a tentative sniff. It smelled like a sea breeze. I placed the first candle back on the shelf and wound my hand to the back of the display, selecting one the color of a toasted almond—definitely a mixture of honey, cinnamon, and vanilla. Maybe some sweet candles weren't too bad. I was hungry for a snickerdoodle just smelling it.

More banging came from the back. Metal tinged against glass, and a hint of rose or something floral drifted out from the back.

"Almost done. Make sure you check out the lotion too."

I hadn't noticed the lotion. A dozen tiny white pots with dainty wooden spoons lined the triangular shelf tucked into the back corner next to the cash register. I scooped a tiny sample of Peppermint Pleasure and massaged it into my palm, immediately rewarded by a faint tingle.

And an unexpected memory. I'd smelled this before. A long time ago.

I distinctly remembered this scent, accompanied by giggles. I was standing in someone's bathroom. A bathroom I didn't recognize. A little blond girl stood next to me, running almost-crimson lipstick along her lower lip.

Running footsteps sounded in the hallway. A boy a few years older than us paused in the doorway. His too-blue eyes flashed as he gave an annoyingly cocky smile. "You know Mom's going to kill y'all when she finds you in here."

"She's not going to find us." The little girl turned to the boy, sticking out her tongue.

"She will if I tell her." He laughed, raising an eyebrow, and sped out of the doorway.

"Don't you dare!" My red-lipsticked companion knocked a tiny white jar of to the floor as she took off to follow the boy. I stooped to pick it up and some leaked onto my hand.

It was this lotion. I was sure of it.

My ears started to ring, and the edges of my vision blurred. I fought for the rest of the memory, but it faded away as quickly as it appeared.

"Reese! So glad to see you! Let me guess—you're here about the lights. Or lack of lights?" Shelby wrapped her arms around me in an enthusiastic hug, and I was startled for a minute. My family tended to be of the personal-space variety.

"Pretty much, yeah. But I can see yours are on."

"Happens all the time." Shelby gave a disgusted shake of her head. "Which is why I have a generator. I kept trying to tell Kate she needed to get one, but no. Nothing could

185

convince her she needed one. Not even working in the dark. You'll have to add that to your list."

"My list?"

"Of updates to the store for when you reopen it."

So we were back in when-I-open-the-store territory. Shelby seriously needed to understand that just wasn't happening. "That's going to be someone else's job. Two more weeks, and I'm out of here."

Her eyes sparkled like she knew a secret I didn't. "Two weeks. That soon?"

She was humoring me. That wasn't going to fly. "Thanks for letting me know about the power." I wasn't staying to play this game. "I'll just have to light some candles or something."

"Don't go quite yet. This is the first time you've set foot in the store. Let me show you around." She rested a hand on her hip, turning to the display like a proud mom pointing out her child at a dance recital. "What do you think of the mint? It's my best seller."

"I can tell."

"You saw my candles."

Shelby escorted me past the checkout counter, and something caught her eye. She gasped in apparent horror. "Do you have your ticket for the Black and White Ball?"

"I have no idea what you're talking about."

"The ball." Shelby spoke the words with such reverence I was almost embarrassed that I didn't have a clue what she meant. Her accent was reaching levels I hadn't heard before, and I'd quickly learned that she used that Southern charm like a weapon. So why was she using it against me? "You have to go."

"I wasn't planning on it."

"But you can't skip it. I mean, you're into history, right? You can't get more historical than the ball." Her eyes gave me an I-can't-believe-your-mother-raised-this-child look, but she gave her best attempt at hiding her disbelief. "Well." She took a breath, and her Southern drawl turned itself up three notches. "The Black and White Ball used to be called the Night of Remembrance. Does that ring any bells?"

"Nope." I wanted to roll my eyes...but I didn't. Shelby seriously overestimated my memory—or my mother's dedication to discussing Devil's Vale history.

She continued. "At the end of the War Between the States..."

"You mean the Civil War?"

"If you'd prefer to call it that, then yes." She shook her head, her blond curls spilling over her shoulders. Not a hair was out of place. "Anyway. As I was saying..." she paused, waiting to see if I was going to interrupt again.

I held a finger over my lips and nodded for her to keep talking.

"As I was saying, at the end of the war, many of our boys were coming home. But one of the women received the troubling news that her husband wasn't. My grandma told the story that most of the men around town expected her to give up the farm, but she wouldn't hear of it. Her grandparents helped found this town. She wasn't going to let a little thing like losing her husband make Annabelle give up the house and land where she had lived since she was just a baby."

"Annabelle? Annabelle Polk?"

"Yes. See. I knew your mama must have told you about it."

"No. It's not that. I saw her picture in an album I found at Kate's."

Shelby let out a loud huff, reaching to her neck and taking hold of a charm on her necklace. I'd never seen the necklace before. She must have kept it tucked under her blouse. The charm appeared to be made of the same stone as the beads on my bracelet. "What kind of stone is that?"

"This?" She pulled the necklace out where I could see it more clearly. "It's called a bloodstone. I guess because of the red. There's a vein that runs through the hills not too far from here. You have a bracelet with bloodstone beads, don't you?"

"It was a gift from Kate. At least I think it was. I found a box with my name on it."

She laughed softly through her nose. "Poor dear. Probably forgot where she'd left it. She was getting a little absentminded in her old age."

"That's what I thought too."

Shelby shook her head as if trying to shake off a fly. "But we were talking about the ball. All the original families are there—the Waters, the Graves, the Polks. You can't miss it."

"I'll probably be gone by then."

"It's Friday. Unless you can wave a magic wand and finish that mess at Kate's, you'll still be here." Shelby spoke with such authority that I had to wonder if she'd been the captain of the cheerleading squad. She was apparently accustomed to bossing people around. "Tell you what. I'll meet you at your house tonight. We need to find you a dress. I'll be there at six."

ß

Shelby knocked on the door at exactly 5:59 p.m.

"Now certainly in the middle of all of this, there's something suitable for you to wear. I remember...."

Ignoring the mess, she marched up the stairs, heading straight for the bedroom to the right of the master bedroom.

She was a woman on a mission.

"When I was little, I actually spent quite a bit of time here. I remember a collection of dresses that your aunt used to have. I always wanted to play dress up, but she never let me touch them. Now let's see."

The door opened with a squeak. I'd have to ask Colton to work on it when he came over next. I turned and looked at the clock. He should really have been here by now—not that I was really keeping track of the time.

"Let me see." Her words were muffled as she pawed through the closet. Coats, shawls, and suits that reeked of mothballs tucked in the pockets whisked past as she dug through the virtual trip through time. "When I played dress-up, she kept them..."

She disappeared into the depths of the closet. I prayed that nothing in there was alive.

"Really, it's fine. I don't need a dress." I raised my voice and waited, hoping that she would give up and just leave. I wasn't in the mood for a ball—not today, not tomorrow, and not even on Friday.

The clothes rustled on their hangers. Something was definitely moving in there. I was thankful I knew it was Shelby right then. Her flats squeaked against something rubber on the floor of the closet.

"Here we are. This would be perfect." She held out a charcoal gray dress like she was the fairy godmother and I was Cinderella. "It's even from the right time period."

"It probably won't fit."

"You won't know if you don't try." All she needed was to stamp her foot and her impression of a stubborn toddler would be complete.

"All right. But I'm pretty sure it's not going to fit. " I took the dress from her hands, finding myself immediately in evaluation mode. Silk, handmade—judging by ever-so-slightly uneven stitches—definitely from the Civil War era. I couldn't imagine how much this dress must be worth on the market. "This isn't a reproduction. How old is this? I can't wear this."

"Sure you can. It's why the Polks kept it."

"To wear to the ball?"

"Isn't that reason enough?" Spoken like a true debutante.

I stepped out of the room and retreated into the safety of the hall bathroom. I inspected the dress more closely, not caring what Shelby wanted me to do. I still wasn't going to damage a dress with such potential historical significance. A day spent digging through Aunt Kate's collections, and this was the first item of value I'd found.

Correction. The first item of potential value that *Shelby* had found. And she wanted me to wear it to a ball.

Granted, it was a ball with deep meaning to the town. If I called my mom, I'd probably get a lecture on "this is why I told you to listen to the stories I told you when you were little." You'd think if my great-great-grandma Polk died on some long-remembered night, I would have heard something about it.

I unfastened the first of the mother of pearl buttons. There had to be at least thirty. No wonder the well-to-do ladies of the time period had ladies' maids.

The fifth button from the bottom had been sewn on with a gaudy pink thread. Definitely not period appropriate. Shelby must have been right. Again. Someone in the Polk past had worn this dress—judging by the faint hint of perfume, not too recently, but definitely not back during the post-Civil War era.

I dropped my clothes to the floor, thinking this dress was definitely not designed to be worn with my current bra. Still, I stepped into the dress, careful not to tear any of the underskirt.

"Do you need some help?" Was she psychic? Of course I needed help getting myself in the dress.

"Sure." I hesitated as I opened the door. We'd reached the point where I felt comfortable describing her as my friend, but we hadn't reached sharing-a-stall-in-the-dressing-room levels of friendship. I spun to turn away from her.

She was faster at doing the buttons than I had been. I could tell she had years of practice dealing with buttons no larger than the tip of my pinkie.

"All finished." She patted my shoulder. "And let's put your hair up. A cultured young woman of the time wouldn't have hair down." She tugged a hair elastic from around her wrist and gathered my hair into an attempt at a bun. "Well, turn around. Let me see."

She smiled. But she wasn't simply smiling. A hint of something else hung around her eyes.

"What's wrong? Doesn't it fit?" The light in the bathroom was so dim, I couldn't quite make out my reflection in the mirror.

"No." She forced a debutante-ready smile. "You look lovely. It fits like it was made for you. Here. Come see." She took my hand and led me back into the bedroom.

I went to stand in front of the full-length mirror tucked into the corner. Even I didn't quite recognize myself.

She was right. The dress did fit like it had been made for me. It curved perfectly over my hips and darted in at my waist, tight enough to reveal every curve but not so tight that I couldn't breathe. It was cut a little lower than I'd like. Lower than was probably proper back then.

"Is this..." I eyed the cleavage I hadn't really realized I'd had.

"Fits just like it was intended to." She crossed the room and tugged my bra straps down, tucking them under the edges of the puffy sleeves. "I'm sure she has a corset in there somewhere too."

I stared at the mirror again. If I didn't know better, I'd swear I'd just stepped back in time. With the lace and silk, it looked like I'd just stepped out of the 1840s. I slid my hand over the skirt with an odd sense of déjà vu.

"What's wrong?" Shelby's face lost the hint it had worn just minutes before.

"Nothing." I hadn't realized just how pale my face had gotten. "I just... I think I've seen this dress before."

Instantly, she snapped back to her normal cheerful self. "Well, of course you have. You've been pawing through all those old albums, haven't you? This is a family heirloom. You've probably seen this dress in pictures before."

The cuckoo clock downstairs announced seven o'clock. Just like that, the spell was broken.

"Oh my." Shelby shook her head. "I hadn't realized it had gotten so late. I'm sorry. I have to go. I have a planning meeting to attend."

"I understand." I didn't understand. She'd been at the house for five minutes, marching straight up the stairs, grabbing one dress, and now was announcing her departure.

Of course, this was far from the weirdest thing I'd experienced since coming to town. The door slammed downstairs, and I knew my time with my fairy godmother had come to an end. She'd helped me pick out my dress for the ball, and now her work was done. I stretched an arm behind my back, tried to reach the topmost button, and realized I had a definite problem.

Chapter Sixteen

Colton

God, how could unpacking boxes make my neck so stiff? I leaned to the side, waiting for the welcome pop. How'd I go from a first string quarterback to a guy who can hardly move after rearranging his office? How'd I even end up with an office at all?

And I was late. After promising Reese that my new job wouldn't affect the repairs on the house at all, I hadn't worked on it at all today. Maybe I could work on the shower after we finished dinner.

A plume of dust was flying up the driveway. I twisted the steering wheel to my truck to get out of the way. To get out of Shelby's way? I rolled down my window and came to a stop. She read my glare.

"What are you doing here?" I leaned out the window, eating more than a hint of dust and dirt kicked up from beneath her car tires.

"Just being neighborly." Her voice oozed with fake Southern politeness.

"You wouldn't know neighborly if it bit you in the ass."

"Careful, Colton. What if Daddy were to hear you?" She batted her eyes with practiced ease.

"Don't change the subject." I'd had a long day. I wasn't in the mood for her games. "Why were you at Reese's house?'

"I was paying her a visit. She needed help finding a dress for Friday. And why are you so protective of her all of a sudden? You haven't known her for even a month. Does Daddy know you're interested in a Polk?"

"I'm not being protective. I just didn't want you bothering her."

"Why, brother, dear, would I be a bother to anyone?" Shelby cocked her head to the side and pressed her hand to her chest, faking injury. She paused for dramatic effect. "Anyway, I came at Mother's request. We have to have a Polk at the Black and White Ball."

"Damn it." I thudded my head against the seat. I'd forgotten about the ball. "I thought that was back in April."

"No, it's not. It's part of Heritage Days, just like it's always been."

"When is it?"

"Friday, like I was just explaining to Miss Polk." Shelby pointed over her shoulder in the direction of Reese's house.

"Her name's not Polk. You know that, right?"

"Well, she's the closest thing we have. There's no way that she's going to have all of Kate's matters sorted out by then. So she'll be here. Reese has to be there. You'll talk to her, won't you? And you know, we've never had a ball without one of the Polks present."

"Well, there's a first for everything."

"Not where the Ball is concerned." Shelby waved a fly out of in front of her face. "And anyway, I even found her a dress. So it's settled. She'll be there." She reached down and closed her window without another word.

Of course it was settled. Shelby got what she wanted. Shelby *always* got what she wanted. It was uncanny, really. Even the most spoiled brat I'd encountered at school hadn't been as adept at convincing people to do things her way.

The dust billowed over the hood of the car, and I watched as my sister's convertible sped down the gravel driveway. She'd never admitted to just how many speeding tickets she'd earned through the years, but I suspected she had enough to consider collecting them a hobby—unless she batted her eyes and they went away.

Why was Shelby really here? Something about the tone of her voice made my skin crawl. She was up to something. No way was she here just to get Reese to come to a party. Keeping to tradition wasn't that important.

But this was Devil's Vale I was thinking about.

Of course tradition was that important.

I parked the car in my usual spot under the tree, glancing up toward the house. No sign of Reese. That was unusual. I didn't exactly expect her to be looking out the window, waiting to greet me after a long day's work, but I could normally could see her moving around in the living room or the kitchen.

She was home, so I felt weird about using my key. Instead, I knocked and waited. And waited.

If Shelby hadn't said she'd just spoken to Reese, I'd have assumed that she must have been working late at the antique store. Shelby said they'd just been rummaging through closets, so Reese must be in here.

Digging through closets. Damn it.

Half of those rooms still had so much stuff in them that they should be condemned. If Shelby convinced Reese to go in one of the death-trap rooms, who knew what might happen.

"Reese!" Still no answer. I reached into my pocket and pulled out my keys. "Hey, Reese. I'm coming in."

I hoped she heard my warning. Didn't want to give her a heart attack.

A muffled voice said something in reply. I couldn't even hear it well enough that I could be sure it was her, but no one else was in there. I whipped around, studying the surrounding lawn. No cars other than her truck. She was definitely in there alone.

I pushed the door open, surprised at how loud it squeaked, considering I'd just oiled the hinges on Saturday. "Reese?"

"Is that you, Colton?" Her voice came from upstairs. My heart churned, trying to prepare itself for what I was going to find. I dug my phone out of my pocket, ready to dial 911 just as soon as I could see how badly she'd been hurt. I cursed Shelby for leaving here alone—and for convincing her to go on the scavenger hunt in the first place.

"Where are you?" I jogged up the stairs with the intensity of my defensive backs during a drill. Unlike them, I couldn't find my target. Which room was she in? "Did something fall? Are you stuck somewhere?"

"I'm in here." Her reply drifted through the bathroom door. With relief, I realized her voice didn't sound hurt. No edge of pain accented her words. If anything, she sounded...kind of annoyed.

Yep. She'd just been hanging out with Shelby.

"Everything okay?" I stood just outside the bathroom door, not wanting to really think too hard about the multitude of reasons she might be in there, besides the most obvious one. "You get locked in?"

"In a manner of speaking."

Now I was confused. "Do I need to help with the door?"

"No. The door's fine." Her voice had an edge to it I hadn't heard before. "It's just..."

Something rustled. Even through the door, I could hear her letting out the kind of exasperated sigh I was familiar with hearing from my mom after a day spent shopping for pageant gowns for Shelby. The knob turned slowly, and the door opened a crack.

"I'm stuck." I couldn't see Reese, but I could hear the defeat in her voice.

"Stuck?" I waited for the door to open more than a centimeter. "You don't have your toe stuck in the bathtub faucet, do you? Because that's out of my expertise."

"No." The door opened a whole inch. I could see a hint of Reese's annoyed expression. "Definitely not that."

"Well then, I can probably help."

"It's much more embarrassing." I could almost put my fist in the crack in the door. Reese looked fine. And then my eyes drifted down to her bare shoulders. Damn, I thought I'd been joking about the bath.

"I'm the guy you introduced yourself to by knocking me out in the chicken coop. How much more embarrassing can you get?"

"Trust me."

She turned her back to the door as it swung open on its uneven hinges. She hadn't just been called out of the bathtub. She was still wearing the dress Shelby must have been talking about.

Shiny gray fabric fit her like a glove...a very well-proportioned glove. It left her shoulders and much of her back exposed, the fine beading showing off her waist like a trophy. The skirt swirled over the floor. I'd seen a lot of women in my days of attending the Black and White Ball, but no one looked like that. And I was just looking at her back.

"I'm stuck." A faint pink color drifted over her shoulders. She was blushing.

Oh, now I understood. Shelby got her dressed up and then disappeared, leaving Reese as a literal damsel in distress.

"I can't reach the buttons."

I swallowed.

As much as I hated to admit it, the thought of helping Reese out of her clothes had already played a starring role in one of my dreams. Maybe more than one. But it was after a night of dinner and maybe a stroll through a park or even a movie. Not...this.

"I can help."

"You don't have to." She peeked over her shoulder with such a conflicted and innocent expression I almost wanted to do much more than just help her with her buttons. Those doe eyes were going to kill me.

Maybe I could think of an excuse to run through the shower. A very cold shower.

I shook my head and held up my hands, trying to diffuse the tension, and draw her eyes as far away from my waist as possible. "I'm your handyman, remember? You tell me what needs doing, and I'll do it."

I just never thought helping her undress was going to be on my to-do list.

"This is awkward. I'm so sorry." She bent her head down and hid her face behind her hands.

"It's not a problem. This is definitely not the first time I've done this."

"Now you're bragging?" Her laugh was like warm butter spreading across toast.

"I have a little sister." Hadn't Shelby told her who she was? I took hold of the top button, and she jumped as my fingers brushed the skin of her back.

I stepped over the pile of clothes she'd left on the floor before Shelby's impromptu fashion show—jeans and a sweater. Perfect. I just had to think about what she looked like when she was in her cleaning mode.

Picture her with these clothes on. Definitely not how much I wanted to see a puddle of clothes like this on my bedroom floor.

I cleared my throat and tried to think of anything. Anything other than the creamy-white skin exposed in front of me.

Passing games. Yards run by the highest-scoring team in the district last year. Not tackling. Definitely not tackling.

"The buttons are kind of small." She apologized to the wall.

"Make sure you hold onto the front of that dress." I realized how much I wanted her to forget to hold the dress.

She was a neighbor, one who needed help getting out of a dress.

A neighbor I'd almost knocked to the floor and had sex with in the middle of her antique shop in broad daylight. I felt a twitch just below my belt buckle.

I worked faster. Who designed these things? No one needed thirty buttons to hold up a dress like this, unless the dressmaker was just trying to increase the anticipation of getting the wearer out of it.

God, I was going to hell for this.

"All done." My voice cracked as I unfastened the last button, and I caught a peek at the hot pink bra strap crossing her back. Not what I expected her to be wearing beneath the conservative gray sweater. "I'll go check on that kitchen sink. It seemed like it was running slow. I'll...let you get dressed."

"Thanks." Her voice was soft as I closed the door behind me.

I needed ice water. Now.

By the time I heard her footsteps behind me, my head was safely situated inside the refrigerator. Neither one of us had to look at the other. I tried to tell myself I was saving her the chance of embarrassment.

But I knew that was a lie.

"Thanks." Her feet shuffled against the floor. I could picture her, standing there, probably leaning against the doorframe. She'd have that thoughtful look on her face, biting her lip and twirling a strand of hair between her fingers. "I'm not exactly sure how that happened."

I couldn't resist taking a peek to see if I was right. I peeked out from the shower stall, and the first thing I saw was her licking her lower lip.

It was worse than I'd thought it would be. I forced myself to look away from her again, and I told my memory that it could stop replaying the feeling of her skin beneath my fingertips. I did *not* need that right now.

"I mean, one minute, I was explaining why I wasn't going to the ball. And the next I was in the bathroom stuck in the dress. I told Shelby I didn't want to go, so why was I even trying it on?"

"Because Shelby wanted you to. She has a way of getting someone to do what she wants." I was going to have a serious discussion with my little sister.

"That's true." Reese leaned forward and rested her elbows on the kitchen cabinet. "She's not what I expected."

"And what were you expecting?"

"I don't know." She laughed, looked at the ceiling, and her eyes twinkled beneath the canister lights above the sink.

"Sure you do."

"Well, Aunt Kate never spoke very kindly about any of the Waters."

"Not about *any* of them?"

"Well, their son seemed to be a decent guy, but he's away at school now."

"At least there's one decent member of the family."

"Exactly."

"But the rest?" I couldn't help it. I was dying to hear how Kate had described my dad. She'd been the only person in town I'd ever seen stand up to him.

"Well," Reese lowered her voice to little more than a purr. "She said they were just really used to running the town." She giggled. "I always thought Mr. Waters would be like J.R. Ewing on *Dallas*."

"Isn't that before your time?"

"My mom loves that show. She watches it in reruns."

"J.R. That's what Ross Waters must be like?"

"They both have an R in their name."

"That they do." I conceded the point. "So, did Shelby convince you?"

"To go to the ball?" Reese traced her fingers along the edge of the tile. She looked like she'd rather be back on the topic of what Kate had said about my family. "She said that there's always a Polk there."

"Your aunt always liked the parties."

"You've been to one?" Her eyebrows shot up so high they threatened to disappear beneath her fringe of bangs.

"Don't look so surprised. It's Devil's Vale. Everyone goes to the party." I was getting in too deep. Of course I went to the party. It was at my house. But I couldn't tell her that. Not now. I should have told her the first night I met her. And now I was stuck. I couldn't go with, *Oh, by the way, I'm related to those people that you seem to be predispositioned to dislike.* "What do you say? Will you be there?"

Reese pursed her lips and a devilish twinkle came into her eyes. "I don't know. I don't exactly have an escort."

She was flirting with me.

Christ help me, but Reese Polk who was really Reese Everett was actually flirting. Did I want to be her escort? Hell yeah.

"How rude of me." I stood, doing my best Rhett Butler imitation. I folded one arm across my waist and made a half bow. If I'd been wearing a hat, I would have tipped it. "Reese Polk, will you do me the honors of accompanying me to the Black and White Ball?"

She blushed again. Seeing the flush of pink on her cheeks was even better than watching it slide down her neck and across her back. "You don't already have a date?"

"Actually, I don't."

"I'd love to." She took my offered hand.

Keeping up the *Gone with the Wind* impression, I brought her hand to my lips and lightly kissed the back of her knuckles. "I'll pick you up at 6:30 on Friday?"

She nodded, blushing even a deeper shade of pink.

This was about to get very, very complicated.

Chapter Seventeen

Reese

"Not again." I sat up, expecting the chords of the piano to have dragged me out of my sleep yet another night. But it wasn't the piano this time. This time, I heard voices.

Not just a few. Probably dozens, low and soulful.

I grabbed my robe off the foot of my bed, ignoring the hiss I earned from Franklin at being disturbed from his sleep, and slid into the sleeves before tying the belt at my waist.

As much as I didn't want to go to the window, I couldn't help it. The voices were drawing me. Pulling me. Preventing me from staying still.

I pulled back the lace curtain, and a shiver running down my spine. It was as if the song was intended just for me.

Despite the darkness enveloping me, I half expected to see someone. Anyone. Maybe even a group of ghostly singers. But there was nothing but the fog. It reminded me of the first night I'd driven into town. That night, the fog had seemed alive, determined to prevent me from driving into town. Now it crept, crawled, and swirled below my window, moving in time with the music.

This wasn't natural.

Unless I was living in a Stephen King novel, fog didn't bend and sway in time with voices so filled with despair that I was almost overcome myself. My body swayed along with them. I could feel the music in my bones. I recognized the song. Kate used to hum it at night as I was going to sleep. Back then, she'd told me it was an old spiritual. Then she'd glanced at the bedroom door, lowered her voice, and explained that was civilized talk for a slave song. They sang of their sadness. Their voices cried out for deliverance.

That was then. This was now.

And these singers wanted deliverance too. A deliverance they thought only I could provide.

The voices were coming closer...closer—coming for me.

I was sure of it.

When I'd encountered the little girl ghost at Daze Gone By, something had snapped. I'd finally broken through. I still might not have found the ghost in the house, but it didn't matter. My disguise had faded. They could see me now. Or at least they could sense me.

Franklin launched himself from the bed with a fury I'd never seen before. One paw caught the edge of the curtain, and I was pulled from whatever spell I'd been under. I couldn't hear the voices any longer, but I knew they were still out there.

Looking for me.

My cat's eyes were keen on me, wild in a way that suggested there was a reason my mother had insisted I bring him on this trip. I backed away from him with the same sense of dread as I'd first approached the window.

I looked at the clock—three a.m. The witching hour. Again.

The singers weren't coming back tonight. I don't know how I knew it, but I did. Still, that didn't mean I'd be able to go back to sleep.

Chapter Eighteen

ॐ

Colton

I double-checked my hair in the rearview mirror before I got out of my mother's car. I was nervous, and it wasn't because she'd made me promise to bring the car home without a scratch. I couldn't even remember the last time I was nervous on a date. But something seemed different about tonight. It didn't feel like just a date.

Maybe it was because I'd caught a glimpse of Reese in the dress.

Or maybe it was because I wanted to help her take it off again.

Christ, I had to stop thinking about the hint of skin I'd seen and how much I was kicking myself for not acting then. A few minutes' more hesitation while I unfastened the buttons of her dress, and the night would have ended much differently. Sometimes I hated my mom for raising me to be a gentleman because my thoughts that night had been decidedly less than gentlemanly.

I slid out from behind the wheel and tried not to slam the car door. No need to alert the neighbors I was here. Of course, I was one of the neighbors, and the rest of my family had practically bullied Reese into coming tonight. They just didn't have to know she was my date. At least they didn't need to know it until we walked through the door together.

I was kind of looking forward to seeing my dad's face.

As I approached the porch, I was surprised to discover Reese already standing there waiting for me. She looked even better than I'd imagined. Her hair was up in soft ringlets. I recognized Shelby's handiwork. I'd wondered where my sister had disappeared off to today. Now I knew.

A subtle blush colored Reese's cheeks, drifting down her neck, and lower than I could allow myself to study. All I could think about was sliding that hint of a sleeve off her shoulder, revealing what the tight corset enhanced right now. If I stared too much, we weren't going to make it to the ball. She gave a faint laugh, and I wondered if she could read my mind.

"What?"

She grinned broadly. "You're in a tux."

"That's kind of the dress code for a ball."

She hesitantly took a step down from the porch, and I reached up to steady her. "This is why you're supposed to let me come to the door. That's what an escort does."

"I was nervous." Her cheeks deepened to an almost impossible shade of red. "You're in a tux."

"I think we've already established that."

"I've just never seen you in anything other than a t-shirt and jeans."

"I'm from Devil's Vale. I think they fitted me for my first tux before I could crawl."

"That would be adorable."

No, she was adorable. The way she was giggling nervously, I had one question to ask. "How many dances have you been to?"

She arched an eyebrow but kept her mouth tightly closed.

"Please tell me this isn't your first dance. Because this is, like, the most boring social event of the year."

"I went to prom."

"That's reassuring." I held the passenger door open for her as she wrestled her skirt into submission. Thankfully, this wasn't my first time driving someone with a dress as large as a small car. Shelby taught me to leave the seat pushed as far back as it would go. "Let me help."

I knelt at the side of the car, helping her manage the hoop skirt.

"Please tell me all the girls wearing something like this."

"Most of the skirts are even bigger, if that makes you feel better." We finally won the battle, and I shut the door before the skirt escaped again.

Reese was ready with a question as I took a seat behind the wheel. "How do they manage to walk in these?"

"Practice. They teach a class at the Preservation Society."

"You're kidding."

I shot her a look that said I wasn't.

"You're not kidding. Y'all really take your history seriously around here."

"Wait until you see the reenactment."

"Reenactment?"

I made sure the car doors were locked before I answered. "That's why it's so important you were at the ball. We had to have a member of the Polk family. It's tradition."

"Please tell me I don't have to do anything." She was reacting only slightly less freaked out than I'd thought she would. "Because no one told me anything about a historical reenactment."

"Nah, it would just be weird not to have someone from every family. Someone might call your name. You might have to wave. No big deal, really. I promise." I surprised myself for reaching for her hand. I gripped it, hoping I could calm her down a fraction. "All you have to do is stand there. The kids from the drama department at the high school do all the rest. It's apparently a big deal to be chosen. They rehearse for weeks."

Reese seemed jittery the entire ride. I couldn't really blame her. Ending up in Devil's Vale during Heritage Days would be enough to send all but the most intense history buff flying out of town. As I'd expected, the iron gate at the end of Preservation Hall's driveway was already open. While we wouldn't be the last to arrive, we were also far from the first.

I glanced in Reese's direction as we joined the line of cars waiting in the valet line. She looked like a toddler watching fireworks on Independence Day—shocked, entranced, and just a little bit afraid.

"First time here?" I didn't need to hear her answer to know it would be yes.

"I didn't know places like this still existed." She craned her neck, staring back at the fairy light-strung oak trees lining the road. We were still too far away from the house for her to get a good view. "All the ones I've visited have basically been rubble."

"That's what you get when you do renovation. Here in Devil's Vale, the Preservation Society takes things kind of seriously."

"I can see that." She leaned forward in her seat. Preservation Hall was just coming into view in all its antebellum glory. The two-story house was massive. Two of my family's houses could have easily fit inside it, and it likely could have held three of Kate's. I'd never been with anyone when they saw it for the first time. "Has the whole house been restored?"

"Not restored." I parked the car as one of the valets approached. He held the door open for Reese then came to take my place at the driver's seat. I pocketed the receipt before walking to Reese's side and offering my arm. "Preserved. Nothing here has ever been allowed to fall into disrepair."

"Can we look around tonight?"

"The rest of the house is normally closed off. We just use a portion of the lower floor tonight."

Reese's face fell. This was probably as close as she got to anthropology-major porn.

"Perhaps we can make an exception for you." Mrs. Carter's voice came out of nowhere. Her wooden heels clicked on the painted wood of the porch, and she came into view, standing above us in the flickering candlelight on the porch. "I'm so happy you agreed to come. It wouldn't have been the same without a Polk."

A cold wave of uneasiness rippled through me. The way she'd been standing there, now turning as if she planned to escort us inside the house—it seemed like she'd been watching us...waiting to see if Reese arrived.

"I do hope you have a lovely time." Mrs. Carter strode away as soon as we stepped onto the porch. If I didn't know better, I'd swear she let out a sigh of relief.

Chapter Nineteen

Reese

I allowed myself one last glance back at the overgrown oak trees surrounding the house. In the darkness, they seemed more like sentries standing guard—the Spanish moss draping down like battle-weary flags, giving little question as to which side of the battle they endorsed. Caught in the filtered moonlight, the myriad shades of gray suggested this wooden army supported the darkness more than any human faction of the war.

"You made it. I was beginning to think you'd had other plans." Shelby swept into the doorway with a little-too-excited smile on her face. If I didn't know better, I'd have sworn she'd been hiding in the shadows on the edge of the porch to wait for us.

But why would she have done that? This was a party. And the little time I'd spent with her suggested she was made to mingle, chat, and dance at events like these. A true Southern belle, she'd been trained for nights like this from the time she could walk.

A strange shadow of a memory played in my mind. Shelby, but not Shelby. A Shelby who couldn't have been much older than five rushed through a doorway at Kate's house, her feet clunking in heels that wouldn't come close to fitting her for a decade. Her lips were cherry pink, and she'd made an attempt to put her hair in a messy bun. Three pearl necklaces practically dripped off her neck.

"Reese, you're not doing it right." She chastised me with a gloved index finger.

"Reese?" A hand pulled at my elbow. I blinked to find Colton craning his neck down in my direction. "Is everything alright?"

"Fine." I shook my head to drive the last whispers of the vision away. Apparently I was already making quite an impression, just not the kind I wanted

The french doors stood open, and what sounded like live music poured out to greet us. From the sound of conversation coupled with the number of cars scattered among the parking lot and circular driveway, the historic house was packed. Exactly what I didn't want.

I took Colton's hand, allowing him to escort me into my idea of hell.

Nothing exploded when I crossed the threshold. Not that I really expected it to, but a weight had been hanging heavy on my shoulders. While I couldn't put my finger on it, after having so many people say that a Polk simply had to be at the ball, I'd wondered if something magical would happen.

Not Cinderella magical. More like Voldemort and the Death Eaters.

I allowed myself a single deep breath, mainly because it was all I could manage beneath the corset. One of the last branches of the Polk family tree had arrived, and the house was still standing.

And what a house.

If someone ever wanted to shoot some kind of sequel to *Gone with the Wind*, this house could be a set. From the grand circular stairwell in the entry to an expansive ball room, complete with a dozen glowing crystal chandeliers, this place was a picture of Southern elegance. I'm not even sure it could be considered a house anymore.

I'd worked on the early stages of restorations in Louisiana. I'd even had the chance to visit a few of them after completion. Those places were ugly stepmothers compared to this one. None of the guests seemed to appreciate the historical opulence around them.

"Are we going to just stand in the foyer?" Colton gave my arm a gentle tug, pulling me back to reality.

"Sorry." I flinched. "Places like this are just dangerous."

"Oh, you won't find anything dangerous around here." Shelby appeared out of nowhere, playing the part of the butler who scared everyone out of their wits in a horror movie. She inclined her head to the side, winked, and gave a stage whisper. "Unless you count the punch. A couple of glasses, and you won't be sober until next week."

"I'll remember that." Colton's hand tightened on my arm before he and Shelby exchanged a strained glance.

Oh great. Now I finally understood why he was dating me and not her. They were exes. And not the friendly kind. Without another word, he led me toward the room on our left.

I wanted to ask something about Shelby, but I also didn't want to know. We were treading in *don't ask, don't tell* territory here. If he didn't tell me, I wasn't going to ask.

"I thought you might like these." He waved a hand toward the far wall of the room. I couldn't guess what the room was once used for. Maybe a dining room. But now it was definitely the historical part of the Preservation Society. Framed documents, photographs, and paintings hung on the length of the wall that must have been at least thirty feet long.

My heels made an echoing clomp as I crossed the marble floor. The first framed document was the city charter protected by thick glass. The swirling script was difficult to read, but I could make out the last names of the three original signers: Graves, Waters, and Polk. No real surprise, but it was still hard to realize that a member of each family had lived here since the city's inception.

Colton stood back, giving me time and space to study the history of town. Occasionally, I caught a whiff of some of the hors d'oevres a tuxedo-clad waiter carried past the door, but when I got in study mode, my appetite switched off. Probably just as well, since I wasn't sure if I'd be able to swallow even a single cup of the punch while wearing this corset.

I paused in front of a familiar face—mine.

My resemblance to Annabelle Polk gave me pause when I looked at the photo in the family album, but seeing it here on the wall made a shiver run up my back. If Shelby hadn't been exaggerating, and most of the town had attended one of these balls, most residents had likely seen Annabelle.

How many of them had to take a second look when they met me?

"Y'all could be twins." Colton approached slowly from behind. I turned back to look at him, but his attention was fixed on the painting. "It's uncanny."

"I don't know," I lied. "I've seen plenty of boys who are dead-ringers for their dad's baby pictures."

"Still." He squinted at the painting before fixing his eyes on me. "It's unexpected."

"How is it unexpected? Haven't you seen it before?"

"No." He appeared to be legitimately confused. "This one's new."

217

Before I could ask any more questions, a bell rang from somewhere else in the house. A somber waiter stepped into the room and dimmed the lights. He cleared his throat, appearing to be waiting on something. "It's time, sir."

"Great." Colton said the word as if it were an expletive. "We're not going to get out of this." He offered his arm, leading me back across the foyer into the ballroom. The guests had already formed an oversized circle, rimming the walls and leaving the center clear for a cluster of nervous high schoolers. "Here goes nothing."

"Good evening. Thank you for joining us." A broad-chested man in a tuxedo that pinched at his waist stepped into the center of the group. He turned in a tight circle, apparently greeting each guest in turn before he paused, his bird-of-prey sharp eyes fixed on me. I flinched, recognizing the man I'd met outside the library. His stare raised goosebumps on my skin. "Now that we're all here, it's time to begin our annual Night of Remembrance."

"Years ago, a deep sorrow fell on our town." A young man wearing a suit at least a size too small spoke first. "After many months of fighting for our freedom and losing so many of our boys far too young, the battle between the States came home."

Another boy moved forward. This one was older, wearing a suit that fit, and his hair was smoothly gelled to the side. His blond hair and blue eyes were almost as light as Shelby's, and I wondered if this was the other member of the Waters family.

"It wasn't enough that her husband had been the tragic victim of a bullet in a faraway field. No, Annabelle Polk was at home with her baby one night, and a stranger, Big Joe, arrived. A runaway fleeing his master saw her house and thought he'd found an opportunity to hide. But she found him. And like any true Southerner, she wasn't going to let Big Joe take refuge in her house. She got out her shotgun and stepped out onto the porch to defend what was hers."

"And defend it she did." The only girl in the group spoke up. Her freckles stood out starkly against her skin, making me wonder if she was that nervous or genuinely that pale. "She fired a warning shot into the air, telling him she meant business. If he was a smart man, he'd leave before she had a chance to reload."

Almost-electric prickling ran over my skin. Fingernails on a chalkboard had nothing on the sense of unease that rippled over me. Every fiber of my being told me to run, but an unseen hand was holding me here, rooted to the spot. I doubted I could move even if I wanted to try.

It's a lie. A voice that wasn't a voice whispered into my ear.

The first boy continued the story. "Jeremiah Waters was tending to his team out in the field. He heard the gunshot coming from across the way. Lickety split, he ran into the house and got his brother, Abraham."

It's all a lie. But you know that already. I could almost feel the brush of someone's breath on my cheek. I jumped, drawing a cutting glance from the woman on my left.

"Abraham and Jeremiah got there just in time." The second storyteller took over. "They found Big Joe standing just feet away from Annabelle. She was kind of heart and didn't want to take a human life, but she would if she had to do it."

"Annabelle stood there. Pointing the gun at the larger man's chest, not even the slightest tremble in her hands. Her daddy had taught her well. She was going to defend her house or die trying." The girl paused, glancing in the first boy's direction.

"But she was also a mother. Her baby cried out, distracting her."

You know the truth. At least you once did.

"Joe took his opportunity. Annabelle was brave, but she wasn't a match for him. He grabbed the gun and spun around to face the Waters brothers."

"The gun went off, dropping both brothers with a single shot. They say Annabelle's scream was heard in the next town over."

It's almost time, child. The time for you to remember the truth. My knees threatened to buckle beneath me. I knew this voice. Kate's voice played over and over in my memories.

And it's time for everyone else to remember you.

Absolute stillness came over the crowd gathered in the ballroom. I might have had question upon question about the story I'd just heard, but it was clear these people drank it in like established history. If someone breathed too loud, they'd be shushed.

Slowly, with the same reverence as I'd once seen at a military funeral, the man who'd started the retelling moved to stand next to a low table with three unlit candles at the far side of the room.

"And now we light a candle for the lives lost on that horrible night. One for Annabelle Polk. Miss Reese, as the Polk family representative, will you come do the honors?"

Every person in the room turned to look at me. No wonder they needed a Polk. I didn't *do* being the center of attention. Still, I couldn't exactly turn him down. Time slowed as I crossed the massive space. If anyone had missed the fact I was a Polk, they knew it now.

My fingers trembled as the man handed me a small butane candle lighter. I fumbled with the starter, much to the amusement of some of the younger teens in attendance. Finally, I was rewarded with a glowing flame. I held it to the fresh wick, a flame erupted almost instantly. The scent of sage wrapped around me. I wondered if Shelby had provided the candles.

"For Annabelle." The man's voice boomed.

"For Annabelle," the crowd echoed.

"Stay here." He rested a hand on my shoulder, holding me in place. The man dropped his arms to his side, surveying the crowd solemnly. "And now it's time to remember the fallen heroes. As the senior member of the Waters family, that task traditionally falls to me. But tonight, I pass that responsibility on to my son."

I glanced at the young storyteller, but he didn't move.

"Colton, come light the candles." Mr. Waters' eyes stayed fixed across the room. For an instant, I thought it was unusual to have two young men named Colton. Then I saw who answered his father's request.

Colton—*my* Colton—stepped away from the wall, his face a mask of guilt and confusion. He wouldn't look at me. That was just as well. It kept me from launching into him right then and there.

How dare he? All this time, after all our conversations, he'd never told me he was one of *them*.

A bitter, metallic taste rushed up the back of my throat while I stood there, playing a role I'd never wanted. He took the lighter from my hand, and his hand brushed against mine. I heard a click, and the candle flickered to life.

"And now we remember." I thought Colton's father uttered the command, but I couldn't be sure. Everything around me faded into sepia, and the ringing in my ears blotted out any sound.

I was moving toward the doorway, not even sure why.

221

A hand caught my wrist, and I turned back, already knowing who it was.

"Reese, wait. I can explain." His mouth moved as if he were yelling, but his words were as quiet as a whisper.

I didn't stop. I needed to get out of the house.

And I needed to do it now.

I made it to the threshold before the world seemed to pitch around me. Memories and half-memories mixed with visions, clouding my reality. I didn't have time to process them. I was too busy being angry with Colton.

"Stop." He'd grabbed my upper arm, and I skidded in my heels. One hand rested on my shoulder as he pushed me back against a wall just inside the front door.

"How could you not tell me?" It took all my concentration to focus on him.

"I was wrong. I get it. I can explain."

"You lied to me."

Pain filled his eyes. "I never lied."

I could feel the veins in my neck straining against my skin. I felt like a volcano ready to explode. "But you didn't tell me the truth. That was just as bad. You are the boy we talked about. When I said Kate trusted *him*... she meant she trusted you."

"So trust me now." His pleading words caught the attention of a few guests milling around the foyer.

"Your drama is drawing a crowd." Shelby swept in, taking command. "We'll deal with this later." Her head tilted, and her eyes locked onto me. "You need to go."

"I'll get the car." Colton moved toward the stairs.

"She's coming with me," Shelby corrected. Somehow she sensed I was too unsteady to walk. She practically steered me over the gray porch tiles and down the stairs. My foot touched the crushed stones of the walk, and Shelby turned back to face him. "I'm the only one who can help her right now."

ß

"You heard them last night, didn't you?" Shelby waited until her car was well-away from the ball before she spoke. But even without words, I'd been able to see the change in her, as if a disguise had melted away.

The Shelby I'd known had been some kind of act. Until now, I'd only met the Shelby she'd pretended to be.

"The singers," she prompted, "you could hear them."

I'd just had a very public fight with her brother—the guy I didn't know was her brother until about five minutes ago. I'd just heard their father tell a story that had drawn the town together for over a hundred years—a story that two ghosts whispered were lies. And now scenes from my childhood were playing out in my head like a movie out of control.

The voices that seemed to be coming for me last night were pretty far down on my priority list.

"I don't know what you're talking about." I'd been trained well—deny, divert, lie if I needed to.

But never, ever tell someone what I could do.

"Don't play dumb with me. It doesn't suit you." Shelby's voice lost its Southern-debutante charm. "I know you heard them."

"I still have no idea what you mean."

She steered her car to the side of the road, throwing it into park. "Look. I don't know what they've done or who did it, but I know what you are."

And from the look on her face, she wasn't lying.

"And now you remember too." She said it so simply that it was clear she knew the answer. "They had to do it. You were too young. It was too dangerous."

It was as if the car had driven into an oven. Sweltering didn't even begin to describe it. This dress and corset had been uncomfortable most of the night, but now I couldn't breathe. Beads of sweat rolled under the scoop-neck collar and down my back.

"Reese, it's time for you to remember. The little girl you remember. The one you played with. Who do you think she was, Reese?"

"She was you." I wasn't sure if I'd spoken loud enough for her to hear me, but she nodded. "But how did you know?"

"Because I never forgot." She reached out and took my hand, anchoring me.

"How?"

Shelby didn't answer. Instead, she waited, simply staring at me with an expression that told me I already knew the answer. My pulse charged like a speeding horse through my veins.

Little-girl versions of the two of us were sitting on the floor of my bedroom. Shelby held a finger to her lips and giggled. Her blue eyes darted around the room, and she tilted her head to the side, listening for any sound. After convincing herself we weren't going to be discovered, she bit down on her lower lip and stared at the candle between us.

224

"You lit the candle." Shelby's secret became clear. "You're a witch."

And then I remembered the sound in the back room the day I drove the spirit away from the little girl. Someone had been in there after all.

"Locks. You were in the storage room. And all the times I thought I'd locked the front door to the shop."

"Guilty." She didn't look too repentant.

Time seemed to stop. I tried to fight a question I didn't want answered. A weight settled deep inside me. "You've always known who I am."

"The spell they used to hide you." She spoke to me as if I were a frightened kitten. "It didn't work on me."

"Why not?" A cold hand ran up my spine.

Shelby ran a hand over her curls, smiling like I'd just walked into her trap. "Reese, honey, I'm not just any witch."

Chapter Twenty

Colton

Dust kicked up by Shelby's spinning tires wrapped around me and filled my mouth with grit. I spat into the dirt before turning back toward the society building. Brilliant lights from the ballroom cast the figure filling the doorway into sharp relief. He shifted, more of his face illuminated.

My father was smiling, grinning even. His eyes were bright like a child who'd just been granted his birthday wish.

I charged his direction, feeling a roar building in my chest. My goal in sight, I didn't even notice climbing the short flight of stairs. Before he realized what was happening, I gripped his tuxedo jacket with hands shaking so hard that I had difficulty keeping myself from throwing a punch.

"What the hell was that?" I shoved him into the doorframe, and he let out a satisfying grunt.

"Not here." He spat the command into my face as if he was yelling at one of our dogs.

"Tell me what's going on."

My father jerked the front of his jacket down, smoothing it with his hands in the same way he'd prepare for a formal dinner. His nostrils flared like a runaway thoroughbred. He wanted me to think he was calm, but his hands clenching and releasing at his side said otherwise.

Laughter and music tinkled from inside, like nothing out of the ordinary had just happened. No one looked curiously out the doorway. Mrs. Carter stood with a group of society ladies in the foyer, and they were discussing plans for the Labor Day picnic.

My father turned back to peer into Society Building. His eyes seemed to travel down the length of the curving stairway that dominated the entry hall. He nodded in satisfaction, his lips curled into a leering grin. In a move that seemed to be intended to make me wait until he was ready to talk, he shoved his hands into his pockets and rocked between his heels and toes.

Just when I was ready to shake the story out of him, he turned back to face me. "Everything looks just fine in there to me."

"I'm not talking about in there." I closed the distance between us and stood so close that I could feel the heat of my father's breath on my face. "What just happened with Shelby and Reese?"

He inclined his head to the side and winced. "I'll deal with your sister later. She's still under the impression she can stop it."

"Stop what?"

He hesitated, taking a step back to study me. Finally, he nodded. "It's time."

"Time for what?" I was damn tired of playing this game. "Just tell me what's going on."

"Wait here." He turned and stepped back into the building. I almost followed, but he held his hand up to caution me to wait. His finger beckoned another member of the city council to come to his side, and my father leaned over to speak into his ear. Mr. Yocum nodded first to him and then to me. My father's shoes echoed over the marble tiles before he exited the building and jogged down the steps with an uncharacteristic spring in his step. He met up with me and motioned for me to follow him. "You actually did what you were told. That's a first."

Instead of continuing on down the path toward the parking lot, he turned and headed toward the copse of trees south of Preservation Hall.

"Where are we going?"

"You'll see."

Melodramatic much? Rather than following him, I should have gone straight to the car and chased Shelby down so I could begin to repair the damage I'd done.

But I had to know exactly what was going on.

"Why can't you just tell me?"

"Come!" The single word exploded from his lips as he pressed on deeper into the trees.

Trailing behind him might have been my only chance for answers. The key bit into my fist before I released it, letting the cool weight solidify my choice. In his dark suit, he was already blending into the shadows far enough ahead of me that I was losing sight of him.

I took a step off the gravel at the edge of the walk and moved through the too-tall grass at what appeared to be the edge of the property. Back in elementary school, Max and I had played here with a half-dozen other kids from school while our fathers met for some kind of guys-only club.

Whether we were playing soccer, football, or hide-and-seek, we'd never strayed off the well-kept lawn or the grounds immediately adjacent to the house. The woods had been off limits.

None of us had known why.

A few more steps through the overgrowth and I discovered the likely reason. Beyond the stickers, thistle, and assorted threatening weeds, an almost-path was hidden beneath the limbs of the oaks. It was not so well-defined as would be easily discovered, but it was here.

The deep rut was masked by pigweed and vines. Someone would have to know it was here to find it. My father found it with no trouble. Without the path, winding through the ever-thickening trees would have been an exercise in futility. There was a reason slaves used to hide in these woods, and it wasn't just to look for the entrances to the tunnels.

Today, even with flashlights in hand, few in town were brave enough to venture into the woods at night. With only lanterns lighting the way, even the shadows likely once seemed alive.

Twigs snapped off to my right, and I resisted the urge to turn back. I'd followed my father this far. If this was the only way I was getting answers, I had no other choice.

"Is it much farther? I'm kind of in a hurry."

My father stayed silent.

God, I'd messed things up. I could see it from the shattered expression in her eyes. I'd predicted not letting her know I was one of the enemy was going to bite me—I just hadn't expected it to happen in quite such a public venue. "I'm outta here. I've got to go find Shelby and explain to Reese."

"You'll do nothing of the sort." His hand shot out of the darkness, catching my arm in a vice-like grip.

We'd arrived at a clearing. Moonlight filtered through the fringe of trees lining what appeared to be almost a perfect circle—a house stood in the exact center. Not a house exactly. It was bigger than a shed but smaller than a cabin.

A bird cawed and winged through the trees, alighting on something a few feet off the ground. A timeworn stone came into focus. "Are we in the cemetery?"

"Close to it." A door squeaked open, and he disappeared through it. "This way."

This is not a good idea. I followed. I'd been too focused on not losing track of my father earlier, but now my blood surged again, and I was at war with myself—knowing I'd made the wrong decision. I just wasn't certain which one it was. "Now can you tell me what the hell's going on? You have exactly one minute before I'm going after them."

"There are *things* about this town that it's time you knew."

"I take it Shelby already knows about them."

A soft chuckle came from off to my right. "She couldn't exactly be left in the dark." He struck a match, lighting a candle.

"Because you could trust her?"

"Because she's a witch."

As the flame grew, the room came into focus around me. Everything in the room could have come from the set of a B-grade horror movie. "If you don't want to tell me what's going on, fine. But stop trying to make a fool out of me."

"No one is making a fool out of you, Colton. You wanted to know the secret. Now I've let you in the inner circle." He paused dramatically, gripping the frame of an ornately carved chair situated at the head of a table that could seat at least a dozen. "Your sister's a witch."

I waited for the punchline. It didn't come. My father spoke as matter-of-factly as if he just told me my eyes were blue. The look in his eyes penetrated mine as he waited for his pronouncement to fully sink in. I took a step back, circling behind the table to place it between us.

"A witch? But..." I ran out of words.

His eyes narrowed as he judged whether or not I was ready for him to continue. "It runs in the family. At least it did. The Waters hadn't had a true witch for generations—not until Shelby."

My father's lips puckered, and he absently scratched his chin with his index finger. In a move I should have expected, he turned toward a cabinet, opening the door to reveal what I should have expected. His fingers closed around a dusty bottle of bourbon.

"I don't want anything to drink." *Especially not that.*

He glanced back at me over his shoulder, his eyes alight with amusement. "Trust me. You do." A generous amount of amber liquid sloshed into the glass before he was satisfied with his pour. "And you'd probably best sit down."

"I need to go find Reese."

"Not until you understand." An edge came into his voice, and I forced myself to sit in a chair that creaked so badly that I wondered if it could support my weight. "It's not exactly a short story."

He poured a drink for himself before he came to join me at the table.

"To history." The flickering candlelight reflected off the toast I didn't echo. Giving me a suit-yourself glare, he threw back the tumbler and winced as he swallowed the bourbon in a single gulp. "Generations ago, three families settled Devil's Vale. The Polk family, the Graves family, and ours."

"You can save me the history lesson, Dad. I've heard it all before."

"No, you haven't." He let those words hang in midair, waiting until I had a chance to let the weight of them settle in. "The families built a community here. Things were peaceful. No one bothered any of them. They all lived quiet lives."

"Why would anyone bother them?"

"Two of the families were...special." He emphasized the last word, locking eyes with me and nodding. "They'd been chased out of more places than not. No one knows exactly how they'd gave to settle here or why the first Graves joined them. But things seemed to be working out until..." He paused, clicking his tongue.

"Until?"

"No one really knows. One of the Graves men saw something. He went a little crazy. He killed two of the Waters boys. One of the Polk women too."

"The Night of Remembrance?"

"Yep." My father stopped talking, pretending his story had reached its end. I knew it was an act—he was just biding his time, waiting for me to bite. When I didn't, he continued. "After that night, things changed. Our women lost most of their powers, same as the Polks. Most of the Graves just disappeared, and they took some important items with them."

"But Max is a Graves."

"So was his father. Their family came back about fifty years ago. And they brought a warning. A new generation was coming. We just had to wait for her."

"Shelby?"

"Reese."

At the mention of her name, I snapped out of whatever stupor my father managed to drag me into. I had to find her. I had to explain. But first, I needed to understand. "What did you do to her?"

"Me?"

"You. With that little ceremony thing or whatever was going on with the candles."

"I didn't do anything."

"Then what was it?"

"You're going to have to blame Annabelle." He chuckled softly, and I wanted to knock the drink out of his hand. "She made sure your girlfriend was invited back to the party. Then everything would go back to normal."

Blame someone who's been dead for a century. That had to be a record for throwing someone under the bus. "Reese can fix everything. How?"

He shrugged one shoulder and scratched absently at his upper lip with the back of his thumb. "Reese has to explain that. She's the one who told us Annabelle was coming back."

We were going in circles—not even a circle. A maze. In the very center stood the one person I most needed to see. I chucked my untouched drink on the edge of the dusty, oblong table. "I'm going to go find her."

"You do that." He nodded condescendingly. A gleam I had never seen before flashed in his eye. Excitement? Evil? His face reminded me too much of a villain in a horror movie—the one who thought he could control the demons...but ended up dead before the end.

I'd never get that lucky. My hand hovered over the doorknob when I heard my father clear his throat one last time.

"And, son?"

"What?" I didn't bother to turn around.

"You tell Miss Annabelle hello for me. You hear? We've been waiting for her for far too long." My father began to laugh like someone who'd lost his mind. "Oh," he waved a hand in my direction, "and leave your mother's car at the house. We might need it tonight."

Acid pooled in the pit of my stomach. I fought the desire to vomit right then. I couldn't dwell on whatever was going on with my father—at least not until I settled something else first.

Still, I did as he asked. There was no need to risk him getting the police chief after me for stealing my mother's car. In his current state of mind, I wasn't sure what my father was willing to do or say. I wasn't sure if I knew him at all.

In half the time it should have taken, I'd driven across town and parked the car in the center of the circle drive. Someone else could mess with putting it in the garage.

I ran up the winding driveway, cursing my too-slick shoes. Wind whirled around me and blew bits of sticks and dried grass in my face. I ran three miles every morning, hardly breaking a sweat, but by the time I reached my cabin, I was drenched through my shirt and jacket.

Fingers of moonlight were reaching through the trees as I threw my jacket toward the porch. I hadn't slowed my pace—not until I reached the oversized oak tree that I used as a makeshift car port. Then I froze mid-step.

Max's car was gone.

Chapter Twenty-one
ॐ☙

Reese

I wasn't sure which made me sicker to my stomach—replaying what had just happened back at the ball, the mixture of memories bubbling to the surface, or Shelby's driving. If I was the key to some town secret, everyone had better hope it was irreversible, because if she skidded any closer to the edge of the ditch to nowhere, we were both going to die.

"Are you alright?" She took her eyes off the road and cut them in my direction just as a thick grove of pine trees practically jumped into our path.

"Fine."

"You don't look fine. You look..."

"Shelby!" I closed my eyes and pointed to the tree that was about to total her car. My eyelids were clenched so tightly closed that tears streamed down my cheeks. I wasn't ready to die yet. I had unfinished business—I needed to kill Colton.

"We're fine, Reese. You can open your eyes." We were magically back in the center of the road. I hadn't even heard a twig snap against the window. "But I suspect my brother won't be when you get a hold of him."

Was she witch *and* a psychic?

"I'm not psychic." She laughed her sweet-as-honey, Southern-belle laugh. "I just saw your face when my father called him to light the candle. I'm surprised he didn't stop breathing right then and there from the daggers you were shooting his way."

"He should have told me who he was."

"Yes. That's true."

"Why didn't he?"

Shelby let out a long sigh as we finally arrived at the turn leading to my driveway. "I believe he was under the impression you were predisposed to dislike my family."

"I told him what Kate said."

The tension in her shoulders almost relaxed, but just as if she could hear an alarm I couldn't, she was back on edge, wary and troubled. Even though she parked the car next to mine, she didn't immediately get out. Her vividly blue eyes seemed to seek out something invisible to me. "Let's get you inside."

"So I'm just going back to my house and acting like nothing's wrong?"

"I didn't say that. Before we do anything else, you need to get out of that dress."

I couldn't argue with that. I might have just been part of some age-old spell that changed my life as I knew it, but that didn't mean I didn't want to preserve the dress.

Shelby rounded the car and took my arm. She half-dragged me across the dirt and up the steps of the porch. I blinked in surprise at how strong she was. Stirring melted wax all day must have given her muscles I couldn't see. She released my arm and reached for the doorknob.

Her hands were shaking.

"Do you need my key?"

"No." I wasn't sure if she'd even touched the door. One second it was closed. One blink later, it swung open. Franklin sat in the center of the foyer, tapping his tail, appearing to be waiting for us. Shelby's lips formed a tight pucker like she'd just swallowed a glass of lemon juice, and I'd never forget the glare she cast at my cat. "You can let them know."

"Are you talking to Franklin?"

"Yes." Her words didn't hold a trace of irony. Now I knew she'd lost it. "Franklin's a witch's cat. Aren't you, baby?"

She leaned down and scratched him on his chin, earning a long purr before he began to spurt and sputter like a cranky lawnmower. I thought she'd done something to him until I noticed the hair rising on end along his backbone. His focus was fixed on the door.

Shelby almost shut it in time.

A heavy boot blocked her movements. She might have been strong enough to practically toss me inside my house, but she was no match for whoever was pushing the door open. I'd rather it have been a what.

Ghosts I could handle.

I wasn't sure about whoever seemed to be scaring Shelby.

"Come on, Shel. Are you really going to make me stay outside? I've been waiting for you all night." Tall, Dark, and Muscular brushed past Shelby as if she was a porcelain doll.

"Max." She said his name like it was a curse word. "Of course you'd show up now."

"You did invite me." He nodded, and I saw the muscles in his shoulders expand. He'd been big before—bulky, like a linebacker. Tonight, though, he could have taken on any pro wrestler in a match.

"I asked you to help before."

"Before you let things get out of hand."

"Before I did what I had to do."

All these befores flew around me so quickly that I felt like I was in the middle of a tennis match. Their verbal sparring wasn't getting anywhere other than making each of them more and more on edge.

"You really think so?" Max's face was somewhere beyond a shade of crimson.

"Yes."

"But you helped them."

"How do you know that?"

"Because someone got her there. I'm assuming that was your doing."

"My brother helped. Honestly, Max," Shelby answered, her voice icy cold. "Do you think it would have been better to leave this in the hands of my father and the rest of the idiots?"

He was prepared to launch into another tirade, but he hesitated, her words sinking in. "What did you do?"

"They completed a spell tonight. But it wasn't the right spell."

Now I was confused. "Not the right spell?"

"Well, it was kind of right." She looked like she'd suddenly been hit by a migraine. "It did unlock Reese's past. However, that's all it did."

She closed her eyes, and I realized just how tired she seemed. While we were whizzing through the trees as if we were being chased by some type of monster, I hadn't really focused on her—I was too busy holding on to the seat of the car. If given a chance, I had little doubt, she'd drop exactly where she stood.

Fury was replaced by concern in Max's eyes. He reached out and took her arm, guiding her around the remainder of the boxes until he helped her settle on the couch. "You did a spell of your own."

She inclined her head in a hesitant nod. "They were using my candles. Not too hard to do."

"Are you sure it worked?"

Shelby turned to face me, the first hint that either remembered I was in the room since the conversation began. "You see your twin around here anywhere?"

"No." Ghosts might not frighten me. They could be dealt with. The memory of the sheer hatred in Annabelle's expression in that photograph, though—that sent shivers up my spine.

With a satisfied nod, she almost smiled. "Then I think it worked."

"You're positive?" Max seemed determined to push her a little harder than necessary.

Her standard confidence cracked. "No, I can't be sure. Not since I don't have the original grimoire."

"Translation?" The corner of his lip turned up like he was teasing her, but he couldn't be...could he?

"Spellbook." Shelby anchored her elbow in the arm of the couch and rested her head against her fingertips, letting her eyes slowly drift closed. "I had to improvise. It won't last forever, not once they realize Annabelle doesn't seem to be coming back."

"You created your own spell to counteract a spell older than my grandfather?"

"Something like that."

He grinned in earnest now. "You really do deserve to be one of the Holders."

"Holders?" Now it seemed I wasn't just missing out on the history lesson—they were speaking in code around me.

"Of the Bloodstones." Max reached out and skimmed the amulet hanging around Shelby's neck with his index finger before shaking his own right hand. A heavy ring I hadn't noticed earlier dominated his middle finger. He glanced down at my wrist. "I've been told you have Annabelle's."

Judging by the interaction between them, I didn't have to ask how he'd heard about the contents of the box Kate had left for me.

Kate's box. And her letter. And the fact she seemed to know she was about to die.

Too many thoughts swirled together. I was as dizzy as if I'd been boating when a hurricane blew into the gulf. Before I stumbled in place, Franklin hopped from who-knows-where and landed at my feet, giving an urgent purr.

"Reese. What was I thinking?" Shelby leapt to her feet, her momentary fatigue banished. "This must be...overwhelming."

I'd never heard her searching for words in the past. Overwhelming was as good as any. "I'm a bit muddled."

240

"I'll explain. Or I'll try. But first, do you really want to stay in that dress all night?

I laughed, not because I was relieved or anything was funny. I was simply too tired to do anything else. "No, not at all."

"Hold the front." She came to stand behind me. With the practiced fingers of someone who'd likely unbuttoned many pageant dresses, the row of buttons quickly fell open. "Go change. Then we'll talk."

I climbed the stairs that seemed far taller than they ever had in the past. As I made my way toward the room I now considered my own, Max and Shelby spoke softly downstairs. They muttered things that sounded like old friends catching up after being apart for too long. The way Colton had spoken about Max, I'd assumed the two of them were friends—not Max and Shelby. But maybe Colton hadn't seen the two of them like I had tonight.

Why was I thinking about Colton? I had enough on my mind right now without adding him to the list. I slid out of the arms of my dress and let it fall in a heap onto the floor. I was a Holder...of a bloodstone. Was that really a rock or just a creepy name for a rock created by a town that specialized in freaky?

I stepped over the pile of petticoats and hoop skirt until I could reach my jeans. As I pulled the worn denim up and over my hips, I almost felt like myself—even if my skin still felt as if I'd been running my fingernails over a chalkboard for most of the evening. Even my lungs seemed to be tingling with pins and needles. Could that be a side effect of whatever spell Shelby had cast?

Shelby had cast a spell. I wasn't new to the world of witches, but I was still going to have to work to wrap my head around that one. My mother had friends who were true witches. I never expected to have one too.

I'd just slid the white t-shirt I'd been wearing all day over my head when I heard a creaking downstairs that sounded a little too much like the front door opening. Max and Shelby had better not be trying to escape. I rushed out of the room and made it to the top of the stairs before I heard him.

"You sure you want to be here?" Her voice was a mixture of teasing and lecture.

"I need to see her."

I was standing at the foot of the stairs before I even realized what I was doing. "Now you need to talk? Now? What about all those times you were here? You didn't think that maybe one of those times you could have mentioned *your last name*?"

"I was kind of fuzzy the first time we met. I thought I'd told you."

"So you're going with the old you-hit-me-over-the-head-with-a-shovel excuse?" Max stood from where he'd been sitting on the opposite side of the couch from Shelby. He was using the same mocking tone that I used to use with my best friend in high school.

Colton looked like he was the one seeing a ghost.

"You didn't notice my car was gone?"

"I figured Dad had it towed."

Max nodded. "Sounds like something he'd do."

"But how?"

Before Colton fully completed his sentence, a set of car keys was dangling from Max's fingertips. "Spare set of keys."

I couldn't tell if Colton was going to hug Max or strangle him. I knew the feeling. "You never called. Or even returned my text."

"I was busy."

"Not too busy to talk to my sister."

"Who happens to be standing next to you." Shelby gave her brother an indignant look.

"Sorry," Colton snapped.

"I'm not the one you need to be apologizing to." A manicured fingernail pointed my direction.

"Reese." His voice was almost pleading.

"Just a second." I held up a hand to put the whole room on pause. "Tonight's been...memorable. And I want to talk to Colton. Before I do, though, what happened back at the ball—is anyone coming after us?"

"Not right now." Max and Shelby answered in sync.

"When?"

Shelby flinched. "I'm not sure. Maybe a few weeks. It'll take them a bit to figure things out. No one knows I could do a spell like tonight's." Colton winced when Shelby uttered the word spell. He didn't know she was a witch. That was a surprise. "They shouldn't suspect."

"And what happens when they do?" Colton asked the question already on my lips.

"I don't know yet. We need Annabelle's grimoire."

Colton expression made it look like his sister had just begun speaking Portuguese. He really didn't know...not about his family. Apparently that made two of us. "Her what?"

"Spellbook," Max answered quickly, exchanging a glance with Shelby.

"So things are fine right now?" Colton asked, looking between his sister and best friend.

"For the moment," Shelby reassured him without looking completely certain herself.

"Then do you think I could have a few minutes alone with Reese?" He stared pointedly at his sister, ignoring the grin beginning to sweep across her face. "I have some groveling to do."

ß

Shelby and Max disappeared out the door as if they had need for discussions of their own, but I doubted Colton noticed the looks that flashed between the pair. If the door had taken two seconds longer to close, they would have seen Colton grab for my hand or at least heard the first whispers of apology.

"I'm so, so sorry." Colton spoke with more tenderness than I'd ever heard from him. "I should have told you the very first day I met you, but I was afraid."

"Afraid?"

"You didn't seem to like my family. I wanted to get to know you."

"I hadn't said anything about the Waters on that first night. Why didn't you say something then?"

"You can't blame me for that night. I'm pretty sure you really did give me a concussion." He gave a bemused smile. His eyes were so wide and so full of innocence, I couldn't help but start laughing, and he quickly joined in. "So that one's on you."

"I couldn't believe you came back. I mean, I'd practically killed you."

Colton stiffened as if I'd just insulted his intelligence. He reached out and took my arm just below the elbow, letting his fingers slide down over my skin until he was holding my hand. "I'm not sure if I'd go that far."

As we stood there, face to face, he entwined our fingers and released mine before taking them again in what felt almost like a dance. I couldn't help it; I started to laugh again.

"Something funny?"

"I just realized we never danced at the ball."

Colton shrugged halfheartedly, reaching toward me again, this time stroking my cheek with the back of his hand. "We didn't miss much. Those dances are pretty dead...no pun intended." His thumb came to rest on my chin. "We have plenty of time for dances."

"We have plenty of time?"

The pad of his thumb trailed along my lower lip, leaving surging heat in its wake. "You're doing that thing again—repeating everything."

"Sorry." A rush of heat flooded my cheeks.

"No, I'm sorry." His eyes locked with mine, and I was already anticipating his kiss, but he paused just before our lips met. "I lied to you. And I've been lied to enough in my life to know how much that hurts. God, I never wanted to hurt you."

I couldn't form words. All I wanted was his lips against mine. I reached behind his neck and pulled his face to mine. That was all it took. Our lips fit together like we'd been made for just each other.

He sighed against my mouth like he'd found his way home.

I wanted more. He read my mind.

One hand scooped below my rear, lifting me against him while his other hand supported my back. He blindly carried me forward until my back crashed against the wall. That seemed to be exactly what he'd been trying for. Once my back was partially supported, his free hand slid higher, tangling in my hair.

He chuckled softly through barely spread lips.

"What is it?"

"You have no idea how long I've been dying to touch your hair." His fingers kneaded through the waves left behind after I'd unpinned my bun. I tilted my head up to the ceiling, and Colton's lips took advantage of the newly exposed skin along my throat. His mouth opened wider, and his teeth trailed down almost to my collarbone. I couldn't repress a shiver.

He lingered in the sensitive spot at the juncture of my neck, making me tremble.

I reached up and touched his face, allowing my fingers to come to rest on his jaw, drawing his head back up in my direction. His parted lips met mine, and he plunged his tongue between them without warning.

My heart sped, and a heat built deep in my core. A desire I'd spent too much energy fighting raged inside, threatening to overtake me. This wasn't the right time for this, and it definitely wasn't the right place for it.

A stack of boxes fell over in what seemed to be a not-so-silent reminder that we had things to discuss that didn't involve a trip to the bedroom. A second set of boxes crashed to the floor, and the moment was fully broken.

I pushed back, away from him. "As much as I want to..."

"Probably not the best time for this." Every word he spoke was laced with regret.

I took a deep gasp of air. "Probably not." I reached for his hand, unwilling to fully lose contact with him. "We still have this whole...breaking a curse thing."

"Spell," Colton corrected without a hesitation.

"Whatever." Once again, my world seemed to be spinning out of my control. Was I connected to Annabelle because I looked like her, or did I look like her because I was connected to her? Did it even matter?

In the end, I was still the key to...the end.

"Hey." He pulled me tight against him again, and his warmth spread and fought against the chill that had settled over me. "We'll fight this."

"Fight magic?" It sounded as hopeless as it sounded like something out of a children's story. "How do you stop something that started almost two hundred years ago?"

"I may be new to coaching, but I've played football since I could walk." One hand drifted behind my back and settled in the gap between my shirt and my jeans. "I know one thing's key. The strongest team wins." He rested his chin on top of my head, and my hair blew in the faint breeze from each breath. "You and me, Shelby, Max." He paused. "Sometimes I want to kill those last two, but I can't think of anyone else I'd want fighting for me."

"Fighting?"

"Yeah." He brushed a kiss over my hairline. "Because that's what we're going to do. I don't care what kind of spell's out there. Or what my dad and his friends think they did tonight. I just know one thing. We're going take them all on. And we're going to win."

Also by the Author

Playing by the Rules

Secrets and Lies, Book One

Dangerous Games

Secrets and Lies, Book Two

Acknowledgements

Writing is a solitary business, but bringing a book to life is truly anything but lonely. Without my incredibly supportive team, this book would never have made it out into the real world.

First off, I have to say thanks to my group of critique partners, Denise, Amanda, Tony, Gail, and Layla. I can't begin to mention how much I value all your input. I'd also be lost without my pre-readers. My thanks goes out to Eva, Marissa, Layla, and Lisa.

I can't forget my editor, Jeni Chappelle. Even when my schedule threatens to make her schedule a bit daunting, she's been incredibly helpful and supportive.

My hat's off to my cover designer, Regina Wamba of MaeIDesign. I had a fairly vague idea of what I was hoping for in my cover, and she managed to bring it to reality. This cover is so perfect for this book, and I hope the readers agree.

Finally, I have to thank each one of you who took a chance and bought this book. You're the reason I write.

About the Author

D'Ann Burrow once told her preschool teacher she wanted to be a witch when she grew up. That simple comment signaled the start of a life-long fondness of things that go bump in the night. As she grew older, she could most often be found with her nose buried in a book, and she was especially fond of the Nancy Drew series as well as anything by Christopher Pike or Stephen King. Occasionally she'd take a trip to the world of the classics where *The Scarlet Pimpernel* and *A Little Princess* reigned among her favorites. She's lost count of the times she's read *Little Women*.

Today, D'Ann enjoys the world of Supernatural, stories about guys with fangs, and she's seldom met a disaster film she hasn't liked. When she grows up, she'd like to work at the Haunted Mansion. Until then, watching *Ghost Hunters* will have to count as research.

D'Ann writes about secrets people keep. Even the bravest heroine or a guy with a heart of gold has a few skeletons in the closet they'd rather not share with the world. When those secrets get out, things get interesting.

A Texas native, she knows making great guacamole is an art form. As a theater mom, she'll happily chat about Broadway musicals by the hour. Molly and Lizzie, the family furry ones, are frequent stars of her Instagram account.